THE FIFTH LOCK

BECCA LYNNE

ISBN: 979-8-9927758-0-8 (paperback)
979-8-9927758-1-5 (hard cover)
979-8-9927758-2-2 (eBook)

This is a work of fiction. Names, characters, business, events, and incidents are the products of the author's imagination. While some locations are inspired by real places, any resemblance to actual persons, living or dead, or actual events is purely coincidental.

Front cover image by INKBookDesign (https://www.etsy.com/shop/INKBookDesign)

Book design by Becca Lynne.

Book edited by Page Perfectors.

First printing edition 2025.
www.linktr.ee/beccatakesnotes

DEAR LITTLE ME,

WE MADE IT.

AUTHOR'S NOTE

Due to the graphic nature of this book, it is not recommended for children under 18.

This is a work of fiction. Names, characters, business, events, and incidents are the products of the author's imagination. While some locations are inspired by real places, any resemblance to actual persons, living or dead, or actual events is purely coincidental.

This book does have some trigger warnings for mention of cancer, car fire, child abuse (on and off page), death of a parent (on and off page), child sexual abuse, depersonalization, disordered eating, drugging, drug overdose, homelessness, medical procedures, murder, Obsessive Compulsive Disorder, racial inequities (off page), sexual trauma (on and off page + fade to black), sex trafficking (off page), seizures, self-gaslighting, and undiagnosed mental health disorders. Please read at your own risk. If this book triggers any sort of strong emotion, please seek help with your counselor or trusted confidant. The main character in this story struggles with an ED that is fueled by trauma. However, EDs can look different for different people, and not everyone's experience is going to look like Delilah's.

If you or someone you know is in need of services, please reach out to the proper authorities:

MISSING CHILD AND ABUSE HOTLINE: 800-843-5678

MISSING AND EXPLOITED CHILDREN HOTLINE: 800-222-3463

HUMAN TRAFFICKING HOTLINE: 888-373-7888

SUICIDE PREVENTION HOTLINE: 800-273-8255

CRISIS HELP TEXT HOTLINE: Text HOME to 741741

NATIONAL EATING DISORDER HOTLINE: 1800-931-2237

Stay safe and mind your mental health. It is important. YOU are important.

PROLOGUE

C urled in the middle of a dingy, stained mattress lies a girl no older than six. The long hair matted around her head blends into the stains on the mattress that her small frame sleeps on. Her faded Little Mermaid nightgown is clearly two sizes too small. Stick-thin, pale legs covered in varying shades of green, purple, and blue bruises are pulled tightly into her tiny chest. Her bedroom door, once a pristine piece of craftsmanship, is now missing its handle and marred by fist-size holes and covered in unidentifiable stains. It doesn't quite sit flush in its door frame thanks to the hinges being pulled from the wood. The scent of ammonia and stagnant air permeate every inch of this tiny room. The room's only light comes from a single bulb hanging precariously out of the ceiling. A chipped dresser with stubborn drawers that don't quite line up with their tracks sits against a windowless wall. Poking out of the drawers is an assortment of worn-out, too-small clothes. In one corner, a neglected pile of broken toys lies forgotten.

In the hushed darkness of the small bedroom, the tiny child stirs from her slumber, her wide eyes flickering open in the pale moonlight that filters through the cracks of the board that covers the only window in the room. A distant crash echoes through the quiet house, causing the girl to bolt upright in her bed. She clutches her favorite teddy bear, its worn fur offering a sense of comfort against the encroaching fear that begins to wrap around her like a cold breeze, sinking down into her marrow. Muffled sounds of raised voices reach her ears, and her tiny heart begins to race.

The soft patter of her bare feet meet the cold tile floor as she cautiously slides out of bed. She tiptoes to the door, taking extra caution to not to make a sound. Her small body is barely visible among the shadows. As she cracks the door open, a sliver of light spills into her room, revealing a narrow hallway that seems to stretch on forever. She hesitates at the opening, her thin fingers gripping the doorframe. She knows if he caught her spying on whatever is on the other side of the door that he would make her pay. Another crash, followed by a thunderous voice, sends shivers down her spine. She knows that voice—her father's. He is angrier than he has been in a while.

And she knows it is her fault. It was always her fault.

The small child stares through the crack in her door, straining to make out what the cause of her dad's anger is tonight. Did Mom not make his drink the right way? Is he out of his "special sugar" that he keeps in neat lines on the coffee table? She had been screamed at repeatedly to never touch his "special sugar," to not even go near it. The one time she had accidentally bumped the table and knocked the white powder to the floor resulted in him beating her rear end repeatedly with a leather belt. She subconsciously rubs at her backside as the memory flashes in her mind. She couldn't sit for a week and it was hard to keep a straight face at school when she had to sit at her desk.

The air is thick with tension. The longer she stares into the dark hallway, the louder the sounds become. Her breath catches in her throat as her wide eyes fixate on the shadowy scene unfolding in the dimly lit living room. Three tall figures stand in the center of the run-down space in a screaming match.

"I told you last time the price was rising! She's becoming quite the meal ticket!" It's her dad speaking. His booming, gravelly voice is unmistakable from the younger voices he converses with.

"Well the little bitch *bit* me last time! She's a liability for *any* profits if she doesn't right that little mouth of hers!" one of the other men spits. His deep voice instantly sends chills down her spine.

The Bad Men.

The men who lock her away and hold her down while she cries for the pain to stop. The Bad Men that her dad always hands her over to, no matter how much she kicks and screams. The Bad Men who punched her tiny figure when she bit them to make them go away.

But they had not gone away. In fact, all it did was make the pain they decided to inflict on her even worse. She didn't remember most of what happened that day, but she knew that when The Bad Men showed up, she was in for an awful night.

She clamps her hands over her mouth to stifle a whimper as her dad's angry words reverberate off the walls and down to her room. Fear etches across her face as she watches him, unseen, pace back and forth, a storm of emotions swirling around and catching everyone in his wake. His arms beat at the air around them as her dad's and The Bad Men's voices grow louder and louder. The small blond girl's world has become a fragile balance of hiding and listening, caught between the innocence of her teddy bear and the harsh reality of her dad's anger.

"She *better* know her manners next time! Or she won't make it back to you alive!"

The young girl stumbles backward at the threatening words, the boards beneath her creaking loudly. She holds her breath and does not dare move. The sounds in the other room quickly stop and she begins to pray that her dad didn't hear the floor. Maybe the loud pounding of her heart was only in her ears and he didn't know she was spying on his conversation with The Bad Men. She shrinks back from the crack in her door just in time for her dad to peer over his shoulder. Her breath hitches at the thought of potentially being caught.

The voices of all three men soften to an aggressive whisper that she can no longer make out. The young child presses her ear into the gap in the door, fighting to make out what the adults in the other room are still in a heated argument about. She isn't stupid. She knows they are arguing about her disobedience. She knows they are fighting over her "monetary worth," whatever that meant. The voices still and a door slams somewhere in the house. She presses her ear harder into the door jam, trying to hear any footsteps or creaking boards that would alert her to movement.

But there's no sounds to be heard. The house sits at an eerie stillness.

She turns her head to peer out the crack when a shadow quickly passes in front of her. The young girl jerks back, covering her mouth and praying to a God she desperately hopes can hear her that she was not spotted. She holds her breath, staring intently at the door. When the door doesn't burst open, she creeps back to her spying place and cautiously puts her eye back to the opening.

The minutes tick by painfully as she concentrates on the darkness before her. No movement happens in the dark stretches of the hallway and she lets out a sigh of relief. The little girl sits back from the open door, sitting on her heels, the tension leaving her tiny body. Maybe she can sleep and not be so fearful of her dad or The Bad Men dragging her from her mattress tonight. She releases the smallest breath she didn't realize she was holding and lets out a tiny yawn. A false sense of security washes over her as she checks the hallway one last time.

Only this time, she is met with the face of her father, his brow is furrowed and his eyes are darkening with rage. The small child stumbles backward, letting out a shriek as the door slams open, rattling the walls of the house.

CHAPTER ONE

Echoes of a loud, pleading scream have become my consistent alarm clock. I hear them every night without reprieve. I clench my eyes to stave off a migraine that begins to form thanks to yet another sleepless night. All because of my very noisy neighbors. It's never quiet in the apartment next to me, but it gets worse in the middle of the night. I rub my palms rather aggressively over my face to get the blood circulating again before I pull myself out of bed.

I pad across the cold hardwood floors to my tiny dresser. Amidst the grogginess of a way-too-early wake up, I fumble with my dresser drawer and pull out a pair of black leggings with a matching sports bra before heading into the bathroom. The LED lights flicker on in my outdated bathroom, nearly blinding me. You would think after living in the same place for the last fifteen years I would be used to these obnoxiously bright lights the apartment complex insists on having throughout the studio.

Gods, I look like I haven't slept in years.

I *feel* like I haven't slept in years.

I quickly yank on my workout clothes, snag a hair tie off the bathroom counter, and pull my hair into a messy top knot. I pull on my socks and shoes before heading to the kitchen to grab my water bottle from the fridge. The time on the microwave reads three in the morning. I roll my eyes in frustration—up two hours early again. At least I can take my time working out and showering before work. I fire up my stationary bike and load up my favorite workout. It's one of the more challenging virtual classes, but I can stand to work up a proper sweat since I don't have to rush off to work.

Thirty minutes later, I'm dripping in sweat.

Good.

I turn off my bike and, before hopping into the shower, I double-check all the locks to the doors and windows. First is the door to the outside.

Unlock.

Lock.

Unlock.

Lock.

I do this repetitious pattern three more times before repeating the ritual on the two windows in my living room and the one in my bedroom. I'm not sure what caused me to be this way, but I feel like my world is crumbling and unsafe if I don't do this. The safety of my entire world relies on locking everything exactly five times. Before I go to bed, before and after I shower, and after I get home from work. Regardless of the time, regardless of how tired I am, I make sure all the locks are secure. I should probably see a therapist about this, but we all know how the police force views mental health. Besides, it's not like it's affecting my life that much. I do it so subconsciously that it's like second-nature now, and I'm done with the whole routine in only a few minutes.

I strip down in front of the mirror that hangs off the bathroom door and drag my hands over every inch of my flesh, my gaze fixed on the reflection that stares back at me. My body, pale and thin, is a stark image against the backdrop. The bones beneath my skin seem more pronounced, creating sharp angles and shadows that define my frame. My face is wan and without sun-kissed warmth, even living in Southern California. The skin clings tightly to my skeleton, accentuating the slightness of my figure. It reveals the delicacy of my physical form, and, somehow, the fragility that lies within, as well.

My reflection shows a vulnerability, a sense of frangibility that is both beautiful and haunting. I am acutely aware of the frailty of my pale, thin body, as if every breath and movement requires careful consideration. It is a tribute to the gentle balance between strength and frailty that exists within me. My body always seems to be a popular topic at work.

"How can you be so fucking skinny and still be a cop?"

"Don't you eat?"

One would think that I reached the perfect state of a slender and fit—a body that a lot of people idolize—but all I see is the extra weight that hangs on to my thighs and stomach. A constant reminder that I need to try harder and that I will never truly be happy with how I look.

Today, the scars that mark my body seem to be more irritated than usual. My father never would tell me what caused all these marks beyond saying I was in an "accident," and since it's the same story I always heard growing up, I eventually just learned to accept it as the truth. The burns that blistered my feet and my shoulder blades are probably the worst of all the marks, but they've never made me feel any sort of way. Mostly because they are easy to hide. No, the ones that give me the most pause are the burns between my legs, the ones that forever changed the way my womanhood is supposed to look. The scars always remain hidden, but they caused me to develop a severe aversion to intimacy. Especially after my first—and only—sexual interaction in high school where my partner took one look at me without clothes and became repulsed. Then, in typical high school fashion, word spread about my disfigurement. Because of this rumor, one day in gym while we were changing, I heard group of girls giggling behind me. I turned toward them only to be met with a flash of bright light! It turns out that they sent a naked picture of me to everyone in school, and I was too scared to ever trust someone again. This only further fueled my body dysmorphia.

I gently run my fingers over the raised lines that crisscross my skin, tracing the unique contours of each scar. I keep trying to appreciate the "personality" they give my body, something my parents always tried to preach in some version of self-love. They vary in size, shape, and color, creating an intricate tapestry upon my body. Some are thin and faded, blending almost seamlessly with the surrounding skin, while others remain more prominent, their presence strikingly visible.

I observe the texture of my scars, feeling the slight elevation and roughness beneath my fingertips. They create a distinct topography, like tiny ridges carved into my flesh, each one telling a different story that I am not privy to. The ones that are less prominent are smooth, almost imperceptible to the touch, while the more noticeable ones bear a rougher texture, like delicate pathways etched into my skin. Like a painter's palette of muted hues, some of the scars are pale and nearly imperceptible to the naked eye. Others bear traces of pink, white, or even hints of deeper pigmentation. Each scar carries its own chromatic signature, a subtle reminder of the healing process that has taken place over time.

And then there are days that I can't even look at myself while showering. The longer I observe myself in the mirror, the quicker it is becoming one of those days.

What happened to me? Why can't I remember?

And why wouldn't my father ever talk about it?

CHAPTER TWO

Five a.m. Still an hour before I need to head to work. Maybe I'll go in early and get some paperwork done. I grab a black pantsuit out of my closet and neatly fold it into a duffle bag with some toiletries and a comfortable pair of dress shoes. Heels are definitely not my thing, especially since most heels show the tops of your feet, and with the burn scars all over them, I'd rather not. My partner and the guys at the precinct don't know about my scars and I'm still not ready to let them into any aspect of my life. Besides, how would I even field questions about how they happened when I don't even have the answers?

You'd think after working with this precinct for the last ten years, I'd be more open about my home life with the other detectives. Or that I would be more personable with them. Ha. Yeah right. Those blowhards only have eyes for the job and getting laid. Definitely not my forte. I can count on one hand the number of times I've actually hung out with anyone from the precinct after work, and the few times I did try, it was awkward and just full of sexual tension, way too much booze, and having to interact with Jimmy outside of work was emotionally exhausting. Have you ever tried reasoning with a toddler? That's what it is like talking to that asshole. I would much rather slice my own hand off than hang out with him ever again.

I double-check all the locks on the windows before heading out the door.

Lock.

Unlock.

Lock.

Unlock.

Repeat three more times. Always in sets of five. Never more, never less.

I shoulder the duffle bag and make my way down the apartment complex stairs. The early morning air is stagnant from the California summer heat and hangs heavy with humidity. It clings to the skin like a suffocating blanket, leaving no reprieve from its stifling grip. It's gross, but it's home. Despite the boiling temperatures of the summer months, the courtyard is lush with thick, short palm trees and succulents in various terracotta pots. I wish we had some more greenery, but it's hard to keep anything alive when it gets into the triple digits and doesn't rain for months on end. In the stillness of dawn, the noise of the city is amplified. The hum of air conditioning units fills the air, struggling to combat the relentless heat, and the constant whir of fans provides a futile attempt at cooling, as well, their efforts falling short against the oppressive temperatures. In these early morning hours, the offensive, hot reality of a California summer becomes all too evident. It is a time when discomfort reigns supreme, and the desire for cooler days and relief from the relentless torment of summer becomes an unyielding yearning.

By the time I am done with my musings about the lack of greenery around my home, I reach my car, a humble and modest 2011 black Chevrolet Cruze with none of the bells and whistles that most people my age have in their vehicles. With a deep breath, I exert a bit of force and the door creaks open, resisting the release of its captive heat. A blast of hot air engulfs my face, as if I have opened an oven door. It feels as though the temperature inside the car has escalated beyond the realm of human tolerability. Like someone plucked me from the parking garage and dropped me into the deepest circles of hell. The air inside is thick, almost palpable, carrying the distinct scent of heated upholstery and the lingering remnants of the stagnant summer. I slide onto the driver's side seat, thankful the material is fabric and not leather, and toss my bag onto the passenger seat. I crank the AC up as far as it will go, giving it a few minutes to cool off before I slam the door shut.

Lock.

Unlock.

Lock.

Unlock.

I breathe a sigh of relief when I am finished with my locking ritual. My father said that I have been doing it since he and my mother adopted me as a child, but never explained why. I don't believe there was ever a need for them to do so, as their actions have never influenced my emotions regarding the matter. They might not have even known why. It was just a "thing" I did—a habit I picked up before being adopted, I guess. Nonetheless, it is a compulsion that my thirty-five-year-old self just can't let go of.

The drive to the precinct at this hour is quiet by San Diego standards. The brick buildings seem to narrow in on the streets in the faint light of the early morning, casting long shadows that stretch across the pavement, making the world around me feel ten times bigger. As the sun begins to rise, the city streets are bathed in a soft, warm glow. The cityscape is still and quiet, devoid of the hustle and bustle that characterizes the later hours of the day. The amount of cars on University Drive is exponentially less around this time, but if I had left even fifteen minutes later, I would have hit the morning rush hour and my typical ten minute drive to work would take double—sometimes triple—that length of time.

As I reach the precinct, I see a squad car parked in front of the homeless encampment that sometimes pops up on the other side of the street. The lone tattered gray tent has seen better days, as has the man who resides in it. His name is Jericho, and he is a long-time family friend that stuck around the area, even after falling on hard times post-military retirement. He was the only person who stayed with my mother after she had been hit by the car that killed her, and my father and I are forever in his debt. I just wish he would let us help him get on his feet. I sigh and shut my door, shouting out to the two uniformed officers harassing the elderly unhoused veteran.

"Hey Jimmy! Why don't you leave him alone? That man has bled for your right to be a douchebag. The least you could do is show him some respect."

The old man and Jimmy exchange a quick glance before Jimmy produces the biggest eye-roll he possibly could. *Gods, he's so dramatic.*

"Shut the fuck up, Jackson. Go do your weird locking fetish bullshit and mind your own business." He slips something into his pocket and storms off.

Jimmy, by most standards, is conventionally attractive. He has thick black hair and piercing golden-hazel eyes. His biceps are clearly visible through his uniform and his five o'clock shadow adds to his chiseled features. I would probably find him attractive if I didn't already know him and find him so fucking arrogant and irritating. His blatant homophobia and racism make my stomach churn every time he opens his mouth. To Jimmy, if you're not a straight White male you're trash. He is the true definition of every cop stereotype that marginalized people fear. Jimmy, of course, never acts this way in front of any of the higher ups and everyone else is too scared to report it to, so he gets away with it. I hate that man with such a passion that any physical attributes that would make anyone else swoon are negated by his shitty attitude. I'm so glad I only see him when I'm at work.

His partner, Jules, is also considerably attractive with his rich, umber skin, beautiful golden-bronze hair, and striking green eyes. I actually kind of like Jules—when he's not around Jimmy, that is. He and his husband, Jake, are some of the sweetest men I know. I honestly feel bad for Jules. Jimmy often takes his prejudices and anger out on his partner, but he just laughs along with him. A survival tactic no doubt. I can only imagine the mental anguish Jules must face having a partner like Jimmy, one that always demeans your existence not only because of who you love but also because of your skin tone. But not rocking the boat means that Jules still has a job, a pension, a home.

Jericho, the unhoused man, seems to vanish from in front of the office. He always has a way to subtly slip into the shadows, probably a skill he acquired from his military training. I hope he's okay and just went to find solace before the summer sun starts baking the city streets.

The concrete steps leading up to the building echo into the still summer air as I walk up to the tall glass building. I buzz the front desk to be let inside and head straight for my locker, slamming it open with more force than I intended.

"Rough morning?" A soft, raspy voice picks up behind me.

"Just Jimmy being his usual asshole self," I respond, my voice dripping with irritation. I close my locker after grabbing my clothes out of my duffle bag, holding them to my body in an effort to dissuade any remarks about my weight. "I don't understand why he is always harassing the unhoused vet that camps across from our parking lot. And why Jules just *allows* it." I pause before finishing my thought. "I honestly don't understand why we're constantly harassing unhoused people anyway. What do we gain from it? What are they doing that harms anyone around them except existing in a way 'we' deem as 'not appropriate'?"

Rita pulls up half of her short black hair before closing her own locker, her dark brown eyes rolling as she speaks. "Because it's our job to protect the citizens...or some *mierda*."

I snort. "Yeah, right. More like protecting the 'image' that San Diego pretends to be for the tourists."

Rita sighs as she heads out of the locker room, having heard me complain about this topic on more than one occasion. "You really picked the wrong field to work in. You know that right?"

I do know that. I knew from the moment I graduated from the academy that I thought differently than my counterparts did. I have always fought for the underdog instead of against them. And I've never understood the way we, as police, act toward the citizens we are supposed to protect. This certainly isn't what we were taught in the academy. We were taught to protect and serve the public, but the more time I serve, the more I realize that most cops' idea of that concept depends on *who* they are protecting.

Jimmy especially has made it clear that that's his take on the job.

As I finish pushing on my dress shoes, Jimmy's remark about my "locking fetish" rings through my ears again. His snide remarks don't usually get to me, but something about them today just crawl under my skin.

Ever since I participated in the Black Lives Matter protests in 2020 and stood to protect those standing for injustice—to protect people like my Dad—my life in the precinct has been hell. Apparently standing for the oppressed means standing against the police. But that's not it at all! I love my brethren in arms (guys like Jimmy being the exception) and I love what I do. Getting the cretins that plague my hometown off the streets gives my life a sense of purpose. However, growing up with a father who is Black has shown me just how cruel the world can truly be when you don't fit the mold the majority has decided upon. Even though my dad was the captain of the exact precinct I currently work at, he has told me multiple stories about how ill-treated he was by his fellow comrades.

Due to my beliefs, making friends with my coworkers is practically impossible. Rita tolerates me since she's my partner, but that is the extent of it. She probably wishes she was assigned someone else but, despite my neuroses, Rita and I make a really well-balanced team and everyone knows it. As far as everyone else goes, I don't need them to like me, as long as I know my conscience is clear and that I do my best to protect the citizens of our town and uphold the letter of the law— if it doesn't interfere with my moral convictions, that is.

CHAPTER THREE

Work has come and gone—a completely uneventful day for my department, something I will always be eternally grateful for. I slip out of the building unnoticed by Jimmy and Jules and make it to my car. Once safely inside, my procedure to lock and unlock the doors takes over. As I'm pulling out of the parking lot, I see Jericho setting his tent up again in the same spot where Jimmy and Jules harassed him earlier.

"Hey! Be careful out here tonight. Sergeant Douchebag is back on shift. I would hate to see you dragged in for something as stupid as just existing."

The gaunt faced man scoffs, "I'm not afraid of that little prick. He'll get what's coming to him eventually."

I laugh, pulling some cash out of my pocket and holding it out to Jericho. "Please take this and go get a hotel room for the night and some dinner." He shakes his head, pushing my hand back. "Jericho, please. It's the least I can do since you won't come stay with me or my dad. It's the bare minimum to make up for my coworkers' disgusting behavior this morning."

Jericho sighs and reluctantly takes the cash I've offered him, a smile playing across his severely cracked lips. "You really are in the wrong line of work."

"So I've been told."

Repeatedly.

*P*lease! No! I don't want to! Please!

You will do as you're fucking told!

I jolt awake, drenched in sweat. Two voices screaming echo through my apartment and keep waking me up in the middle of the night. I am so exhausted from these neighbors constantly fighting and I am really hating these thin walls. Why doesn't anyone else ever seem to hear them? I've begun watching their apartment door when I am home to see if I can catch a glimpse of who lives next door so I can confront them, but I never see anyone. I even knocked on their door a couple times to do an unofficial welfare check, but they haven't answered. Either they aren't home, or they know I'm a cop and don't want trouble. Either way, their constant screaming matches are definitely messing with my already fucked-up sleeping schedule. I flop backward onto the mattress, throwing a pillow over my head, and groan. I just want to get a full night's sleep. Just once. *Please?*

After fighting with the Sandman for what feels like ages, I give up on ever finding sleep. Tossing the pillow aside, I roll out of bed, change into some workout clothes, and make my way to the exercise bike sitting in the corner. If I can't sleep, I might as well do something productive, since visiting hours for Dad aren't for another four hours. I mindlessly scroll through the trainers on the digital screen until I come across the one who will give me the results I want. The HIIT workouts always help me work up a sweat and forget about my problems because it takes everything in me to focus on *not* passing out while I ride.

By the end of the hour, I'm dripping in sweat and breathing hard. My tank top clings to my form and there are visible sweat drip lines along my inner thighs. Just like I do every day, I check all my locks before hopping in the shower for some self-care. I carefully peel off my drenched clothes and toss them in the hamper. The heat of the shower feels wonderful on my aching muscles until...

No! Please! Stop it! Please! It hurts!

I stumble backward and slam into the shower wall banging the back of my legs on the faucet at the same time. I suck air in through my teeth in pain and shake my head vigorously to clear my thoughts. The screaming is so loud, and the pain in the small, disembodied voice makes my heart race. It sounds like my neighbors have a child that I wasn't aware of. I'll have to speak with building management before putting in an official request to Child Protective Services for a child welfare check.

T he elevator dings when I'm on Dad's floor and as the doors open, I am hit with an intense wave of bleach smell. The cleaning crew must have recently made their rounds, which is great for the patients and their care, but man does it make me want to yack everywhere. My flip-flops softly echo in the quiet hallway as I traipse to Room 707, the room that has housed my Dad for the last three months since the cancer became really aggressive. All it took was one grand mal seizure to place him in the hospital and keep him here for what feels like an eternity. I knock lightly—which is more of a formality at this point than an actual to request to enter—as I turn the cold steel handle to his door and poke my head in.

"Hello?" I say barely above a whisper. I push the door farther open. "Daddy, are you awake?"

Something resembling a hoarse croak comes from behind the drab curtain. "Yes, princess. Just watching the news."

"More like the news is watching you, old man," I snort in jest as I kiss his forehead. "How are you feeling today? Have you seen the doctor recently?"

"Not too old to still kick your ass." My dad laughs a deep belly laugh, sending him into a coughing fit. After a few wheezy breaths, he speaks again. "The oncologist should be in sometime today to go over lab work and a better long term treatment plan..."

He trails off and just stares blankly at the television. He used to be the epitome of health. Once a tall, muscular Black man with a clean face and a high and tight haircut, he is now gaunt and ashen. His black hair has turned a dingy gray, bald on the top and patchy on the sides. Even his eyes no longer sparkle. The cancer has been wearing him thin, and the doctor's prognosis for him isn't good, but I keep holding out hope that maybe *this* round of chemo will be the one to kickstart him again. Maybe *this* round will be the one to start kicking the cancer's ass.

Just one. More. Round.

I can't help but hope and pray to whatever God or Gods may be listening to fix him. He is all I have left. My mom, Juliet, died when I was sixteen in a hit and run just three short years after they adopted me. Dad always tells me how she lit up any room she walked into. Mom used to joke that it was because she was a fiery redhead. I don't remember much of my mom in the short span I had her, but I do remember just how madly, truly, deeply they were in love and just how much they both loved me.

I can't lose my dad. Not now. Not when there is no one else for me to rely on. No one to confide in. No one to be my best friend the way my dad is.

No one to love me.

"...did you hear me? Delilah?"

I shake my head vigorously to clear my thoughts that are beginning to spiral. "Yeah, sorry. What were you saying?"

My Dad cocks his head. "I asked if you were all right. You seem thinner than normal. Are you eating?"

"Of course, Daddy," I lie. I don't need him worrying about my eating habits, or lack thereof, when he needs all his strength to combat his disease. "Just tired." At least that's true. The last two nights, I have been abruptly awoken by screams echoing through my apartment, compliments of my neighbors.

Dad glares at me through slitted eyes. He doesn't believe me any time I say I ate unless he physically sees me. For as long as I can remember, I have had an aversion to food, and it was something he and Mom battled with me about for so long. "What's going on, pumpkin?"

I sigh heavily. I can at least talk to him about the nightmares, if nothing else. And Jimmy—that douche bag. "The last two nights I've been having really bad nightmares. But they're...they're different. They feel *real*."

I recount to my dad the last two nights of my neighbors' constant feuding that only takes place in the wee hours of the morning, and how I think the commotion is making its way into my dreams. He sits quietly and watches me intently with his dark-brown eyes, but something stirs in them, something that seems to trouble him. Or maybe I am just seeing things and he is just growing more weary due to the aggressive treatments.

"Oh my god! And then there's the shit with Jimmy at work." I let out an exasperated growl.

My Dad laughs. "Is he still picking on you for your OCD?"

I nod like a sheepish child but then disgust takes over again. "Yeah. And he's constantly harassing Jericho. He camps outside the precinct sometimes. I've tried offering to put him up until he can get back on his feet, but he always tells me no, he'll find his own way."

Dad makes a face at the mention of Jericho. "Del..."

"Do you need me to get you something?"

"No, it's just...you're thirty-five, Del..."

"Ye...yes?" Is Dad going senile to the point where he doesn't remember my age? Where is he going with this?

A look of defeat washes over Dads' face. "Nothing, pumpkin. I love you, just remember that."

I lean over and kiss the top of his balding head. "I love you too."

I move an uncomfortable hospital chair over to the side of his bed and hold his hand in silence as the TV buzzes in the background. We sit like this for a few hours until I start to nod off. My dad nudges me gently.

"Are you okay, Daddy? What do you need?"

"Go home, Delilah. You're exhausted. I'll call you after I talk to the oncologist."

I want to protest, but he is right. I really should try to catch up on some sleep before I go back to work. I kiss his forehead gently, saying my "see you later" and "I love you" before getting back into the bleach-smelling elevator. As much as I want to sleep, after talking about the bickering tenants next to me, my mind is racing. A run is definitely in order if I want to have any hope of getting to sleep tonight.

The walk around my neighborhood is just like any bustling city on a Tuesday. Fast food restaurants serving lunch to hungry patrons, drivers not paying attention to anyone and either slamming on their horns or their brakes. Sometimes both. The San Diego summer sun beams down onto my light skin, causing it to redden and the freckles to become slightly more pronounced. The sights, sounds, and smells are so brutally overwhelming today that I decide to cut my walk short, even though I'm still not tired and I'm not sure I could even sleep with the way my mind is reeling.

As I round the block, I'm hit with the overwhelming stench of Marlboros as I careen into an older gentleman a few inches taller than me. His skin is California-tan with dark hair just barely starting to streak gray. Something about him makes my skin crawl.

He smiles, his teeth stained yellow from the tar. "Sorry about that, miss."

I freeze. My cop instincts naturally take over as I survey every feature of the man standing in front of me. His salt-and-pepper hair, leathery skin, and dark eyes shoot chills down my spine. Something about this man just isn't sitting right in my gut.

The man peers at my face, searching its features—for what, I don't know—and every inch of me erupts into gooseflesh. I can feel my eyes widen as the man looks over me. "Are you all right, miss? Do I—Do I know you?"

I straighten up, a tactic I learned in the academy: *fake it until you make it.* "I don't believe so."

"Surely I do! You look quite familiar...I just can't place it..."

All I can do is shake my head. This heat must be getting to me, because I feel kind of nauseous and dizzy. Can he stop talking already?

"Ah, well, you look like someone I used to know. No worries. You have a good day." And just like that, he walks off, the stench of cigarettes trailing behind him as he lights another upon walking away.

CHAPTER FOUR
VICTIM #1

At one a.m. on a balmy summer night, the city's nightlife is in full swing. Bright neon signs glow above the entrances of bars and clubs, beckoning revelers with promises of merriment and escape. Laughter and chatter spill out onto the streets, mingling with the occasional blaring of car horns in the distance.

The atmosphere is rife with the scent of various beers and cocktails, and the sharp tang of spirits. Groups of friends stumble out of the bars, their cheeks flushed and their steps unsteady. They lean on each other for support, laughing at inside jokes and recounting the highlights of their evening. Some shout loudly, their voices carrying through the warm night air. As the night wears on, the crowd slowly thins out, some opting to conclude the evening and return home, while others venture forth to discover fresh locales or seek out dimly lit corners nestled between alleyways and brick structures, eager to explore their partners' bodies before reaching the comfort of their own homes.

The night air seems still as the streets become mostly deserted, with only a few flickering street lights offering a faint glow. Most everyone has left, creating a stark contrast to the bustling scene usually seen in waking hours. One man in particular becomes the intense focus of a figure clad in all black. The night life continues to carry on around the drunkard, completely unaware of the shadowy figure that follows him. The man so completely oblivious to his surroundings sways back and forth as he traipses his way to his destination, stumbling on the uneven sidewalk.

Deep lines etch his weathered face, revealing the traces of countless experiences and challenges he has faced over the years. His scent is a blend of lingering tobacco smoke and an excessive dose of low-quality whiskey. The color of his faded graphic t-shirt has dulled with time and multiple washes, and the design on the shirt, once vibrant, has now become slightly cracked and worn, adding to his overall disheveled look. It hangs loosely over his slightly baggy jeans which show signs of wear at the knees, suggesting that they have seen many days of use. The cuffs are unevenly rolled up, revealing worn-out sneakers that have seen better days. It is clear that this man is not out to impress anyone or be awarded "Best Dressed."

Time slips silently by as the dark, hooded figure trails behind the man who is still unaware of their presence. The drunk man fumbles with his car keys, his unsteady hands struggling to find the keyhole. He lets out a frustrated sigh as he squints through bleary eyes, attempting to align the small piece of metal with the lock. The keyring, adorned with various keychains, jingles loudly against the quiet hours as he tries to find the right key. His coordination seems to have abandoned him as he continues with one key after another, not having much success. Each time the key misses the lock, he lets out a groan of irritation, growing more impatient and adding a new nick to the paint job with every failed attempt. He leans heavily against the car, using it as support to keep his balance. When he finally manages to insert the correct key into the lock, he turns it with a clumsy twist, but his timing is off and the lock doesn't budge. He tries again, his brow furrowing in concentration, but the key refuses to cooperate. The frustration imprinted on his face only grows and he lets out a slurred curse under his breath. As he reaches for the handle, his hand misses, grasping at thin air for a moment before finally finding its target. With a clumsy tug, he manages to open the door, but his balance betrays him, and he begins to topple forward.

With a sudden lurch, he loses control of his body and falls into the driver's seat, landing in an ungraceful heap. The impact jolts him, and he lets out a groan of discomfort. His arms flail for a moment, searching for support, but they only find the steering wheel, which adds to his struggle. His head lulls backward against the headrest, and he blinks, trying to regain focus. The scent of alcohol clings to him like a cloud, permeating the small space of the car. His hair, a disheveled mop, sticks to his forehead with sweat from the warm summer night.

As he plops himself into his seat, the passenger side door swings open, letting the hooded figure slide into the seat. The newcomer is shrouded in shadows, their face obscured. The driver turns to look, his eyes widening with a mix of shock and concern then shifting to sudden anger.

"*What the fuck?!*" he slurs, but it sounds more like, "*Fusha fu?!*"

The click of a gun as the assailant cocks it and points it at the drunk man's head causes him to turn a ghostly white. He begins to quickly sober up as his life begins flashing before his eyes.

"Please, whatever you want, you can have it! Just don't kill me!" he pleads. Though his words are still slurred, they are a little more comprehensible.

"Drive," is all the dark-clad figure says in response.

Obediently, the drunk man puts his car in drive and starts forward in a slow crawl. He grips the steering wheel with white-knuckled intensity, his fingers tense and almost trembling, the gun still pointed at his head. The veins on the back of his hands stand out, revealing the sheer force of his grip. His knuckles turn pale under the pressure, a clear sign of the stress and anxiety coursing through his body. His face wrinkles with worry, brows furrowed and jaw clenched. His eyes are transfixed on the road ahead, darting from side to side, constantly scanning for any potential hazards or obstacles. Or maybe hoping to see a cop that would notice his suspicious activity and save him from this stranger that dropped into his car.

"Turn right," the voice sharply orders.

Every turn of the steering wheel is precise and deliberate, as he tries to maintain control over the vehicle, as if his life depends on it. Because it does. By this point, the man has all but completely sobered up as he turns down the dark alleyway. Usually the homeless encampments would've been set up all over this part of town, but tonight, there is nothing. No witnesses. No sex workers. Nothing.

"Park."

His hands shake as he parks his car, his heavy breathing causing the smell of the liquor he consumed earlier to filter through the air. It smells like a bar mat in his car—stale, cheap alcohol mixing with the overflow of beer. A nasty but distinct smell. As the drunkard turns to face his kidnapper, the butt of the gun whacks him square between the eyes. His skin splits as blood starts to well to the surface and pour over the bridge of his nose. The driver sees red and instantly forgets that his unexpected passenger has a weapon.

"You sick fucking bastard!" he spits at his passenger. "You'll pay for that!"

Before he has the chance to grab the gun from underneath his seat, the trespasser slams the pistol across his eye, breaking the orbital socket. The now alarmingly sober man lets out a sharp scream as searing hot pain shoots across his face. He reaches his hand up to clutch the injury, grinding his teeth and moaning in agony. The assailant takes advantage of the man's painful distraction and quickly begins weaving a rope around his body and the car's seat, their fingers moving deftly, almost as if in a dance. The driver flails against the rope as it holds him in place, spewing a long string of curse words at the mysterious attacker.

The shadow-clad figure grips at the restrained man's face, using un-natural force to pin the driver's head back against the headrest, their free hand stuffing an oil-soaked rag into his mouth. The pungent stench fills his nose. His eyes widen, and he shakes his head profusely, muffled pleas and cries coming out of his mouth from around the cloth. With blood still pooling down the victim's face and his right eye swollen shut, his aggressor pulls out a handheld torch—similar to the ones you'd find in bake shops for crème brûlée—and lights it.

The attacker gets mere inches from the frightened man's face, a men-acing grin playing on their lips. "Don't worry. It'll only hurt for a minute or two. Probably."

The San Diego Union-Tribune

INVESTIGATION UNDERWAY AFTER MAN FOUND BURNED IN CAR

BRADLEY CHANCLER, 63, FOUND BURNED ALIVE IN HIS CAR BY POPULAR NIGHTCLUB

SAN DIEGO - The San Diego County Sheriff's Department has launched an investigation into the circumstances surrounding an individual discovered dead in a burned car.

According to preliminary information from SDSD, deputies were dispatched to the 800 block of West Washington St in Hillcrest at 2:20 a.m. Sunday morning regarding a vehicle on fire after a concerned citizen called 9-1-1.

When deputies arrived, they located the burning car in an alleyway by The Lamplighter, a popular bar in the area. San Diego County Fire Department personnel responded and quickly extinguished the flames.

Once the fire was put out, an individual was found inside the vehicle. They were pronounced dead at the scene by paramedics, authorities said.

The identity of the decedent has been confirmed to be Bradley Chancler, 63, and his cause of death has not been determined.

Arson investigators and homicide detectives are conducting separate investigations into what led up to the deadly car fire.

CHAPTER FIVE

Please! I don't want to do this! Please! Stooooooooop!

I bolt upright, drenched in sweat, my blond curls splayed across my face. When are these late night arguments going to stop?! And what the *fuck* is that buzzing sound?! I angrily search around my bed until I find my phone, face down in a mess of tangled bed sheets. It's still pitch black outside, save for the faint orange glow of street lamps. The buzzing of my phone at this ungodly hour could only mean one thing: something happened with work that requires my assistance.

"Hello?" I answer without so much as glancing at the phone screen, a bit more agitated than intended.

"Detective Jackson?" The person on te other end sounds as exhausted as I feel. "This is dispatch. We need you at the station right away."

Shit. "Yeah, okay. I'll be there in fifteen."

I hang up and toss my phone back into my pile of sheets, flopping backward onto my pillows along with it. My eyelids flutter closed as I try to prolong the inevitable, yearning for a few more precious moments of slumber. With dispatch's words swirling around in my head, I sigh in defeat and roll out of bed not even five minutes later. I feel like I haven't slept in days and all I want to do is crawl back under the covers until it is time to get up for my scheduled shift. Or, better yet, until I finally feel rested, but the latter doesn't seem likely to happen anytime soon with my neighbors screaming at all hours of the night. In either case, I certainly don't want to come in at...

Three a.m.

SIX HOURS EARLY?!

Ugh. This lack of proper sleep is going to be the death of me.

I walk into the precinct, the heels of my shoes echoing in the silent hallway. Rita, the bags under her eyes a stark contrast to her hair perfectly pulled back as always, comes out with a hot cup of tea and a stern look on her face.

"Drink this," she says as she shoves the foam cup into my hands. "We'll take the sedan. Everyone's already on the scene except the coroner. He's on his way."

I smile into my cup as I follow behind Rita to the parking lot. It's little moments like this that make me think that maybe, just maybe, Rita actually does like me and doesn't just tolerate me. I have only told her once, ten years ago, that I didn't like coffee and much prefer green tea and she's never forgotten. Any time we've had an early morning call, she always gifts me with a cup of tea. I cautiously sip at the steaming liquid as we both slide into the black-on-black squad car.

I hate riding with someone else in the car, but I hate it even more when someone else is driving. I fidget uncomfortably in the passenger seat as Rita puts the car in reverse. I fight tooth and nail to not click the locks five times. I hate that this controls me so much. I dig my nails into my pants and bite the inside of my mouth. I can feel my world starting to spiral knowing I haven't completed my ritual. Rita's side-eye is palpable as we approach the gate that leads from the parking lot to the street.

She sighs, exasperated, and puts the car back in park. "Go on."

She is outwardly agitated this morning that she has to deal with my neurosis. Usually, if my compulsions do bother her, she at least doesn't show it, but today she doesn't try to hide her disgust for being stuck with the "broken cop." I can't help but fixate on the locks, no matter how hard I try, and no amount of therapeutic techniques I've tried has lessened this urge. My skin crawls and I'm not on top of my game if this routine isn't performed everywhere I go that has a lock. I have even been caught fidgeting with locks while on an crime scene. I may do it subconsciously, but it is still something I'm not proud of. Rita has always made sure to hide these blunders when she notices, but I feel that she is getting more and more fed up with having to cover for a neurodivergent partner. We may have been working together for long enough that Rita has □ accepted—more or less—that her partner is always going to have these tics, but it doesn't mean she can mask how she feels all the time.

Maybe one day I'll get around to asking my dad if he knows what caused these compulsions, or if I ever had any sort of testing done before he adopted me that explained them, but today is not the day.

I hurriedly click the lock buttons before thanking Rita, who is already speeding off as soon as I finish the sequence. She knows it by heart nearly as well as I do. Five sets. Ten clicks total. Never more. Never less. As we merge onto the deserted street in front of the precinct, the city lights loom on the horizon like distant stars. My pre-scene jitters always bring a mix of excitement and unease, knowing that I am about to witness the familiar (yet always different) scene of flashing lights, fire trucks, and whatever gruesome act that calls for my attention unfold before me. Rita turns on the radio and we sit in a comfortable silence as we pass by iconic landmarks, their imposing forms softened by the dark. The grandeur of the buildings is not lost in the night; if anything, it feels magnified, as though the city has withdrawn its daytime façade and exposed its true essence to those willing to explore during the witching hours. As we drive on, my mind wanders and I notice solitary figures ambling along the sidewalks, lost in their own thoughts and heading to destinations known only to them. They add a touch of mystery to the nocturnal tableau, and I find myself imagining their stories and the reasons they, too, wander the city's streets at this late hour.

At stoplights, I continue to gaze around, captivated by the serenity that envelops the cityscape, yet knowing full well the brutality that awaits us at the end of our drive. Still, the familiar scenery takes on a surreal quality, and I marvel at how different everything appears when shrouded in darkness. It is as though I have stepped into a parallel universe where time moves differently, where the city has a chance to breathe and reflect. Something that I really need to work on myself. As we continue on, I can't help but feel a sense of connection with the city, as if we are sharing an intimate secret. Driving downtown in the middle of the night feels like a beautiful symbiosis, a dance between myself and the urban landscape, where I am both an observer and a participant in this enigmatic midnight waltz. Except this waltz doesn't end in a beautiful bow by willing participants. Our journey—our waltz with the city—is ending with a crime scene.

As we slow our speed and pull up to the site, my gut is beginning to twist into knots. Something about this area feels all too familiar, a prickling feeling creeping up the back of my neck. There is something I just can't place about the landscape around me, and the unease in my stomach is tough to ignore.

The call on the possible homicide came from a small alleyway not too far from the precinct. The flashing red and blue lights of our squad cars illuminate the alleyway, and despite the late hour, it attracts a gathering of unhoused individuals and those too intoxicated to make their way back home or arrange for an Uber. Rita parks just behind one of the cop cars, being sure to leave room for the bus when it arrives. A familiar figure in the shadow of the car catches my eye. It must be the trick of the light and my tired disposition, but I swear I see Jericho slinking away into the night. I shake my head and try to blink away my exhaustion.

A junior officer, looking a little worse for wear, meets us at the crime scene tape and lifts it up for us to duck under.

"What do we know?" I ask as I lift my head to take in the entire scene.

In the dimly lit alleyway, cloaked in darkness, a burnt car stands as a ghostly sentinel against the night. Its once red paint job is now masked in a sickly, charred black on one side. The acrid scent of burnt rubber and metal hangs in the air, creating an unsettling atmosphere. Firefighters move cautiously around the car to remove their hoses to allow us easier access, trying hard not to disturb any of the potential evidence that was left behind. The surrounding walls and pavement seem to absorb the faint glow of nearby streetlights, casting elongated shadows that shift eerily around the scene. The passenger door is left wide open, allowing anyone in the line of sight an unobstructed view of what took place inside the vehicle. The metal frame is warped and twisted from the intense heat, a visual testimony to the destructive force that consumed it. The interior of the car is a mere shell of what it once was, now reduced to a skeletal framework of melted plastics and scorched upholstery.

The smell of burnt flesh and oil permeates the air as Rita, the junior officer, and I approach the vehicle.

"Not much," he says. "The victim's name was Bradley Chancler. Thank God for IDs, even if they are slightly melted."

Rita cocks her head, slowly peering in through the open passenger side door, "Why's th-" She stops short at the sight of the victim still in the driver's seat.

Or, what's left of the victim, I should say.

There in the passenger seat sits the charcoal remains of what is un-doubtedly a human. The majority of the burns seem to be centralized on the victim's face and torso, but the most unusual part of all of this is that the victim is tied to his seat. It is hard to discern any distinguishing marks on the body, like tattoos or birthmarks, due to the amount of charring. The flame marks that licked at the ceiling of the vehicle have left strips of the fabric scorched and entirely non-existent in other places, exposing the metal of the roof. On the ground in a thick substance are the words "Dead Men Don't Rape."

"Looks like we've got a pretty good idea on motive. Did forensics get a photo of this?" I ask, carefully avoiding stepping on the message as I try to get a closer look at what used to be Bradley's face.

"I think so. They're still processing the scene."

I nod and ask, "Who called it in?"

"Some late night bar patrons called the fire department around one thirty saying that they heard screams coming from the alley and when they went to investigate, they saw the inside of the car on fire. EMS called us after finding Mr. Chancler's body inside the car."

This isn't some random murder. There's definitely something more sinister going on here, given the brutal nature of this crime. I can only assume that, with him being tied to his seat, Mr. Chancler was alive when he was set on fire. This man was tortured, and the message on the pavement makes it abundantly clear why: revenge. He preyed upon the wrong person, and with the victim being so badly burned, it is very doubtful we're going to find any evidence left on his body. Hopefully the killer left some DNA in the car somewhere.

"Did you get any witness information when you got here?" I ask, pinching my nose, trying to rid the stench of singed flesh from my nostrils.

The junior officer pulls out a notepad and flips through a few pages. "Uh...yes. Name and number. I told the witness someone from the homicide department would be contacting them."

I quickly copy the information from his notebook and start to head back to the sedan. "Thank you. I'll let ya'll finish up with the coroners and I'll head back to the station to start digging up any information on Mr. Chancler. He had to have pissed someone off. This was too personal to have been a random killing."

I slump into my desk chair, pressing my head into my palms, seeking a momentary respite from the day's demands. It's only five in the morning. My shift doesn't technically start for another four hours, but that doesn't matter anymore now that we have an active case, and anyway, something about the location of the crime scene is bothering me. My gut is usually right when it comes to stuff like this, but it isn't telling me anything specific. It's just saying that this is...off. I have so many unanswered questions. Why was Jericho lurking around the car? No one else seemed to notice him skulking in the shadows. And was this man really a rapist? There's always the possibility of mistaken identity. I rub my palms into my eyes, clear my throat, and begin to search the database for any information on our victim.

Surprisingly—or maybe unsurprisingly given the nature of his death—his name pops up in an old case file from *twenty-six years ago!*

Man, someone was holding a grudge.

I open the file, and as soon as the page loads and Bradley Chancler's mug shot appears, my skin begins to crawl. *Holy shit!* This is the guy I ran into right outside the apartment yesterday! He's younger in this picture, of course, but a steady unease sits deep within my belly as I stare at his smug expression. I begin to scan his rap sheet in an attempt to start piecing things together. He was only in his thirties when he was booked for...

CHILD SEX TRAFFICKING?!

Disgust immediately runs through me, the hairs on the back of my neck standing on end.

Maybe he did deserve what happened to him.

It says that he was released from prison last year but is still on parole for another two years. Hell of a way to spend your first year free from prison—in a body bag in our morgue.

"Find anything?"

I jump at the sudden intrusion of sound to an otherwise quiet workspace and whirl my head around to see Rita standing behind me holding out a cup of steaming liquid. I graciously take the warm cup from her, taking a sip before placing it on my desk. The hot tea noticeably releases the tension in my shoulders.

Rita's perfectly manicured eyebrow arches. "Everything okay, Jackson?"

"Yeah, just really tired. Sorry. I totally zoned out," I chuckle, hoping it sounds more nonchalant than I feel as I take another sip of her offering. "This guy was involved in some real shady shit back in the day. Child sex trafficking twenty-something years ago. He only just got out of prison last year."

Rita leans over my shoulder, her straight black hair falling in a curtain around her face. "It says here that your dad was assigned to this case but they redacted everything else. Probably for the protection of the minors involved," she says matter-of-factly. "Maybe you can see if your dad is up to talking about the case. See if there's anything he can remember that might help us figure out who mutilated the poor sap."

Poor sap my ass. This guy only went away for twenty-three years for what he did to those innocent children. He got what was coming to him if you ask me, even if it was two decades later. Rita, however, has a point. I should call my dad up and see if he remembers anything pertinent to this case. It might give us a direction in which to go. A lead is a lead.

Even if it's a retired detective.

I pace outside the precinct waiting for my dad to pick up the phone, the hot San Diego summer sun beating down on me. It's almost noon, so he should be at least somewhat coherent. His chemotherapy isn't supposed to be for another three hours. The treatment makes him feel exhausted mentally, emotionally, and physically for at least half the day, if not more, so getting him on the phone beforehand is imperative. I spot Jericho poking his head out of his tent, his gaunt face dripping in sweat. I wave half-heartedly at him just as Dad picks up the phone.

"Hi, Daddy. How are you feeling today?"

His voice is ragged and his is breathing labored, "Ready to go home."

"I know, Daddy, I know." I sigh. I hate knowing he's stuck in that sterile room with no end in sight. "Can I ask you something?"

The other end of the phone goes silent, save for Dad's heavy breathing and the subtle beeps of all the monitors he's attached to. I wait patiently for a few minutes while Dad regains his strength to talk. I hate asking him for anything anymore because I know it takes so much out of him, but it's important I talk with him about this. He was the one who put Bradley Chancler away and, with so much information redacted, any information I can get might point us in the right direction of his killer.

"Anything, pumpkin."

"You remember almost every case you ever worked on, right?" I chew on my bottom lip, afraid that my question will cause unnecessary stress on his already frail body.

"A lot of them still haunt me to this day." His breathing becomes more haggard, so I wait for him to catch his breath before interrogating him for answers.

"Do you remember anything about a child sex trafficking case involving someone named Bradley Chancler?"

Dad goes mute, and if it weren't for the sound of the IV pump in the background, I would've assumed we got disconnected. "Daddy? Are you there?"

"It's not one that I recall." He sounds agitated. He's hiding something. I can tell by the curtness in his voice, but rather deter me, it only makes me more determined to keep pressing him.

"Are you sure? I just need to know—"

"I SAID I DON'T REMEMBER! DROP IT, DELILAH ROSE!" A deep, chest rattling coughing fit ensues after his shouted words.

I flinch at my Dad's sudden burst of anger and use of my full name. He's never lashed out at me like this before, and something inside me crumbles. I can feel tears welling up in my eyes and I all but forgot how to speak. My dad, even at thirty-five, is my hero and my best friend. I've always been the apple of his eye, and I have never done anything to disappoint him or cause him to raise his voice at me. My reaction to his outburst even shocks me.

"I'm sorry, pumpkin." Dad takes a few short, uneven breaths. "The chemo is making me lose my temper. I love you."

I take a deep breath in an attempt to calm my nerves before speaking. "I love you too, Daddy." My voice sounds small in comparison to how it was when I first started this call to him, and a different kind of voice—a nagging voice in the back of my mind—berates me for asking him in the first place. Guilt is now taking over me. "I'll let you go. I have some paperwork to do in the office before I can go home."

We exchange pleasantries, and I hang up. I scan my surroundings making sure no one is around before I squat down and weep silently. The realization that he is slowly failing at life—made painfully obvious by his inability to hold onto a short conversation-awakens dark emotions inside of me that I haven't felt since my mom died. I'm not ready for this to be the end of him. I need him to get better. He's survived so many hardships, so much loss. This can't be the thing to take him down.

I straighten myself up, smoothing out the wrinkles in my blouse, and get hit by the overwhelming stench of cologne and cigars wafting up my nose. The smell is so strong I almost puke.

"Are you okay, officer?" A man with a thick accent appears out of nowhere.

"Ye-yes, I'm—" As I turn to thank the man for checking on me, my chest suddenly tightens. I feel a lump beginning to form in my throat as nausea threatens to overtake me.

"Hey! I know you!" The man's dark face lights up.

"I don't think so?" It comes out more like a question than a statement.

"You're a Henderson, aren't you?"

"No, sir. My name is Detective Jackson. You must have confused me with someone else." I stand tall and square out my shoulders as I proudly declare my allegiance to the name that made me. I haven't heard or even used my dead name—my name *before* I became a Jackson—for as long as I can remember. This is a name I cut all ties to. I never again want to be associated with anything before my parents became my parents. I refuse to acknowledge any part of a past with *those people* who didn't even want me. Anyone who knows me by that last name is someone I want nothing to do with.

"Are you sure? I could have sworn... " He reaches his hand out toward my face, his cigar still perched between his knuckles.

I visibly recoil, a mix of anger and disgust swelling in my chest.

"Well, I must be mistaken. Either way, you're quite beautiful," he coos in a tone far too intimate for a stranger.

Seething rage courses through my veins and I begin to shake. The man, with his balding, salt-and-pepper hair and dark-brown eyes, strikes an indescribable emotion in me, and I can't tell if I want to run or punch him in the face. He steps closer, brushing my cheek with his cigar-holding hand. I lurch backward in disgust, tripping over the uneven sidewalk landing hard on my ass. Something sinister lurks in the depths of this man's eyes as he looms over me. My heart begins to race, its beats echoing loudly in my ears as a feeling of impending doom washes over me. *What is happening?!* My eyes well up with tears as I clench them closed and my chest begins to constrict, the emotions from my conversation with my dad spilling over onto this interaction.

"Hey! Leave her alone!" A booming voice rings out above me. I open my eyes to see Jericho standing in front of me, squaring up on the stranger. "Back away now before I do something we both regret," he growls.

The man throws his hands up and takes a few steps back. "Hey now. I mean no harm. No need to threaten violence."

Jericho snarls, "Then leave." He steps toward the guy threateningly. It feels like hours, but it's probably only a few minutes before the man bathed in cologne turns on his heel and walks off as if nothing happened. Jericho turns to me and reaches his hand out, but I just stare, my body absolutely refusing to work.

"Hey, Delilah...Are you okay?" The old vet's voice is gruff and deep but has a familiar softness to it that offers me some comfort.

I shake my head and take his hand to help pull myself up. "I...I think so. I don't know what happened. I don't think I have ever felt like this before. It was as if all of my training went out the window. The lack of sleep and stress must be getting to me. I'll be fine."

Jericho's face is difficult to read, but I can see the lines there softening in understanding. If anyone understands what it is like to have no control over how your body reacts in certain scenarios, he is definitely that person. I thank Jericho again for his help and walk as quickly as I can to my car before slamming the door shut, breaking down into uncontrollable sobs as I attempt to lock the car with shaky hands.

Unlock.

Lock.

Unlock.

Lock.

Unlock.

Lock.

Unlock.

Lock.

I finish my usual sequence.

Wait. Something doesn't feel right. But why?

CHAPTER SIX
VICTIM #2

Drunkards and happy couples buzz around the streets, the smell of smoke, alcohol, and sex lingering in the air. Inside an upscale restaurant, conversations throughout a lavishly decorated room within the establishment vary in volume, but above them all, a deep, heavily accented Armenian voice is the most recognizable. Supermodel-bodied women with platinum-blond hair in slinky party dresses hang off of his arms. With his signature cigar clutched between his tan knuckles, he drapes his own arm over one of the women's shoulders.

"Tonight, we celebrate!" He laughs boisterously, his companions joining in. What they are celebrating is unclear, but everyone happily slings back glasses of expensive wine like it is water. A waiter, clad in a black-on-black ensemble, appears behind the well-dressed man and whispers something in his ear as they clear the table of all the empty wine glasses. The waiter looks a bit apprehensive to deliver his message, picking at his cuticles as he waits for acknowledgment.

"Friends!" he proclaims loudly. "Someone has requested my attention inside the restaurant. I shall return! Don't let the party stop in my absence." The man plants hard sloppy kisses on the women who have been hanging on him all night. They swoon dramatically, fanning themselves with their hands as he walks away.

He stumbles into the dimly lit restaurant, chuckling with various groups of people and clapping random men on the back as he passes them. The interior exudes opulence, with a masterful blend of rich textures and exquisite materials. Sumptuous velvet drapes in deep, velvety ruby red cascade from the ceiling, adding a sense of decadence to the surroundings. The walls, adorned with tastefully framed artwork and mirrors, reflect the subdued glow, adding depth and dimension to the space. It is clear that this man is well-known and well-loved. Cigar smoke follows behind him, his dark form moving across the room, flashing a grin to everyone he passes. The mahogany wood doors to the kitchen swing open as he pushes past them.

Chefs and sous chefs move with purpose from one station to the next, prepping last minute dishes that came in prior to last call. The stainless-steel countertops are lined with neatly arranged ingredients, ready to be transformed into culinary masterpieces. The overhead lights beam down, illuminating the scene, ensuring that no detail escapes the watchful eyes of the culinary artists. At the heart of the kitchen, the head chef stands tall, orchestrating the entire operation. Clad in a pristine white chef's coat, their focused expression reveals a mix of passion and determination. With a wave of their hand or a nod of approval, they guide their team through the culinary ballet. The tall, tawny-skinned man moves around them with ease, complimenting the kitchen staff as he moves to the back door.

As the door closes and the sound from the restaurant fades, the man is met with the barrel of a gun pointed directly at his face. His eyes widen at the sudden intrusion at his workplace. But all too quickly, the man's face goes from a look of shock and fear to a relaxed, almost jovial look.

"Hey now! My friend. Let's talk about whatever has you stressed." He takes a courageous step toward the gunman. The alley's only light casts harsh shadows across the perpetrator's features, making them unrecognizable. The attacker smirks. They had to give it to him, he was ballsy. Who walks directly toward someone pointing a gun at their face!?

The shooter cocks the gun in an attempt to show that they mean business and jerks their head toward the dumpster, signaling for the restaurant owner to move in the direction they want. The man's brow furrows as he cautiously starts to walk behind the dumpster.

The dumpster itself stands tall and imposing, a large metal container with a heavy lid that shields its contents from view. Its surface is weathered, bearing the scars of countless interactions with garbage bags and waste over time. The smell that emanates from within is an unpleasant mix of rotting food scraps, discarded packaging, and various kitchen detritus. Surrounding the receptacle is a patch of ground littered with debris that has escaped the confines of the trash bags. Empty cardboard boxes, crushed cans, and bits of discarded food wrappers create a haphazard mosaic on the concrete.

Scrunching his nose at the smell wafting from the dumpster, Davit turns to face his captor.

"While I am an equal opportunity kind of man, I'm not really interested in a blow—" the elegantly dressed man starts to speak before the butt of the gun strikes him across the cheek.

The assailant growls, "I'm not looking to suck your cock!"

A sly smile creeps across the Armenian man's face, noticing that he very clearly struck a nerve with the hooded figure standing in front of him. "You might enjoy it. I haven't heard any complaints." He adds a nonchalant shrug as he slowly fiddles with his belt buckle. Looking over his assailant's features, he tries to make out any familiar markings. He focuses on their lips, and his own suddenly curve up into a wicked smirk at the recognition of who is in front of him. "Oh come on. It might be everything you didn't know you were missing."

The gunman, fuming and blind with rage, rears back and punches the man square in the nose, hard enough to break it. Davit stumbles backward into the dumpster, wiping the blood that has fallen from his nose on his upper lip. His eyes flash in fury.

"Oh, so you decided you wanted to be a little *asshole*, did you?!" the man says rabidly, nearly foaming at the mouth. He lunges at the dark figure, drunkenly tripping over his feet, before collapsing to his knees as the butt of the weapon makes contact with the back of his balding head. The assailant kneels on the drunk man's back, grabbing a fistful of his remaining hair, yanking his head backward. Davit's dark-brown eyes are now bloodshot from the blunt force trauma, and thick splatters of blood coat his nose, lips, and chin.

Without another word, the attacker smashes his face into the concrete over and over again until he goes limp, as barely audible groans escape his now misshapen mouth. The music and chatter from restaurant patrons drown out the violent dealings currently unfolding behind the building. Unbeknownst to them, their compadre is fighting for his life. Dark stains of blood decorate the dirty concrete in the alleyway. The malefactor stands up, chest heaving and glowering at the perfectly still body, their eyes cold as night. Only a few distant streetlights dare to break the darkness, painting scattered pools of soft, amber illumination.

The brutalized man rolls over feebly and peers at their attacker, coughing up small spurts of blood.

"You'll pay for this," he grunts out, an evil laugh on the heels of his words, weak as they may be.

As Davit continues with his weary verbal onslaught, the hostility on the killer's face grows with each passing second. They squat down, grabbing their victim's limp body by the front of their shirt, their face inches from the weakened man's.

"Don't worry. It'll only hurt for a minute or two," the black clad figure sneers as they forcefully drop the man back onto the concrete, his head bouncing off the surface. They stand, taking one final look around them before repeatedly stomping on the man's head until it caves in.

The San Diego
Union-Tribune

LOCAL BUSINESS OWNER FOUND DEAD IN ALLEY BEHIND HIS OWN RESTAURANT

DAVIT PETROSYAN, 56, FOUND DEAD BEHIND POPULAR RESTARUANT BY BUS BOY

SAN DIEGO - The body of a local business owner was found in the alleyway behind a high-end restaurant owned by the decedent located at the 4100 block of Park Boulevard Tuesday morning. Officials say the death has been ruled a homicide.

A bus boy who worked for Petrosyan found his boss's body while taking out the trash during closing duties for the local hotspot, Rare Society. According to a police report, the bus boy (who wishes to remain anonymous) said Petrosyan received a mysterious letter around 10:30 p.m. before he disappeared. The bus boy has said it was not uncommon for Petrosyan to disappear randomly for hours on end.

Petrosyan was found with his head bashed in and an eerie message written on the wall behind him in blood, according to the report.

He was dead on the scene and an autopsy will be done to determine the extent of the damage, according to the San Diego County medical examiner's office. Anyone with any information is urged to call the San Diego tip line.

Area detectives are investigating but nobody is in custody.

CHAPTER SEVEN

Yet again, I am suddenly jolted out of a not-so-deep sleep, a mess of tangled bed sheets and sweat. I can feel my heart pounding in my ears and the start of a migraine coming on. Why do I feel like I just ran a marathon? I press my palms against my eyes in a frustrated attempt to regain composure as my phone starts vibrating its way off my nightstand, hitting the ground with a thud. The faint orange glow of the street lamps filters through my window, alerting me that it is either very late in the evening or way too early in the morning. In either case, I should still be asleep. With an exasperated sigh, I lean over the edge of my bed and flip my phone over to see who's calling, the back light from the screen nearly blinding me.

Groggily, I choke out, "Hello?" These early morning calls need to stop. What is it with police emergencies that *always* tend to happen overnight? Can't they do it during normal working hours? I mean…I know they won't, because criminals usually don't want to conduct their less-than-legal activities in the harsh light of day, but still!

"Jackson? It's McGillicutty. We have a situation over by Rare Society. We need you here as soon as possible. Hernandez is already en route."

"So are we just not taking squad cars to crime scenes anymore?" I snap. Jules doesn't deserve my attitude and I quickly apologize. "Do I at least have time for a shower?"

"Probably not. Just shower at the station when you head back. You're going to want to after you see this."

Yeah. No thank you, I think, still rather grumpy from being woken up for a second time this week by a homicide call.

"Okay, Jules. Give me a few minutes to get dressed and then I'll be over." Jules is a nice enough guy; it's not his fault that he's partnered with a jackass. In fact, it really grinds my gears that he ended up with a partner like Jimmy and no one in the precinct seems to notice—or maybe they do and they just don't care—the way Jimmy treats him. I only hope that eventually he can work up the courage to stick up for himself and his husband when Jimmy goes on his rants about how gay marriage should be illegal because it's "not natural" and whatever right-wing rhetoric he decides to spew.

I hang up and glance at the brightly lit screen: three o'clock in the morning. *Again.* This killer is going to have to start finding a different time to get their rocks off because I am so over these early morning wake up calls. I pull on a pair of slacks and a black, long sleeve button up. I am quite possibly going to regret this wardrobe choice later, but that's a problem for future-me. Current-me needs to decide what to do with the blond hair that is more of a rat's nest than curls at this point and without a nice, deep conditioning treatment, it isn't going to be easily managed.

Top knot it is.

I grab my gym bag and make my way out the door, repeating my locking and unlocking habit.

Unlock.

Lock.

Unlock.

Lock.

Unlock.

Lock.

Unlock.

Lock.

Four times, and I start heading toward my car.

Why doesn't this seem right?

J ust like my last middle-of the-night drive to a crime scene, I notice
now that driving downtown at three a.m. is a surreal and captivat-
ing experience. It's something that, despite my recent bitterness about
having to be awake at this ungodly hour, I never take for granted. The
city, which is typically a bustling metropolis during the day, now reveals
an entirely different side—the hushed, tranquil side that emerges only in
the depths of the night.

The streets that are usually crowded with vehicles and pedestrians are
now remarkably empty, creating an unusual feeling of spaciousness and
freedom, something not usually found in the cramped quarters of San
Diego. The traffic lights rhythmically change colors, but there are no long
queues of cars waiting at the intersections. Instead, I find myself driving
through green light after green light with no other vehicles in sight. It
doesn't take me long before I'm pulling up on the scene. Blinding bursts
of the red and blue lights from the squad cars illuminate the alley and
yellow crime scene tape litters the area. Jules, Jimmy, and Rita are all
huddled together watching as the forensic photographer snaps away, the
bright flashes from their camera like lightning against the darkness.

"So what are we looking at?" I interrupt the trio's hushed conversation
as I duck under the tape.

Jules speaks first, exhaustion wearing on his normally poised features.
"Davit Petrosyan. Age fifty-six. Blunt force trauma to the head. We spoke
with the employees of the restaurant who called us around midnight.
They said they received a letter for Petrosyan to meet someone in the
alley around ten thirty last night while he was entertaining guests, but
by the time everyone finished shutting down the restaurant and cleaning
up, he still hadn't returned. They all confirmed that his random disap-
pearances and late returns are common, so no one thought to go look
for him."

Like clockwork, Rita nudges my hands with a lukewarm cup of tea. It warms my soul a little that she still does this even in front of Jules and Jimmy, given Jimmy's open disdain for me. She starts to recite the info she was given by the officers that were first on the scene.

"Bus boy was throwing out a bag of garbage when he found Petrosyan. Poor kid is barely nineteen and found his boss with his head smashed in. That can't be good for the psyche."

"No, no it's not." My words are absentminded. Something about this situation feels...*off.* "Anything else?"

"Time of death, according to the coroner, was possibly only a couple hours ago, probably shortly after he received the note. Maybe between ten thirty and eleven?"

"So this guy was getting his head bashed in and *no one* heard or saw anything?" This piece of information catches my attention and I raise my eyebrow. There's no way a crime of this magnitude could happen in silence. The guy literally had his head smashed open. That is *not* a silent crime in the slightest. Surely someone heard *something.*

I stare around the crime scene. The body lies sprawled in front of the dumpster, varying degrees of blood spray and brain matter littering the surrounding area. Flies have already started to stake their claim on the decaying body. Just like the last victim, written in what appears to be blood on the brick wall behind Davit are the words "Dead Men Don't Rape." A busted open trash bag lies just a few feet from the victim's body where the bus boy must've dropped it in sheer terror. Out of the corner of my eye, a moving shadow catches my attention.

Is that...is that Jericho?! No, it can't be! I blink and the shadow of a man is gone. I must be losing my mind.

Rita tilts her head. "See something, Jackson?"

"I'm...I'm not sure." I shake my head, trying to clear my thoughts. "Did you get any information from anyone besides the bus boy?"

"No, no one has come forward. We're going to have to subpoena the local businesses for CCTV footage to see if they caught anything."

I nod, only half listening. Between the sleepless nights, my neighbors constantly fighting, the early morning wake up calls for this string of murders, and my worry over my dad, the exhaustion is starting to wear on me. And now it's gotten to the point where, for the second time in two nights, I swear I saw Jericho at the crime scene. I shake my head again, hoping to wake myself up a bit. What I really need is a nice hot shower followed by an uninterrupted nap.

And for all this nonsense with the volatile neighbors to stop.

I stare blankly at my computer screen, the cursor blinking slowly in the search bar. I'm supposed to be looking for information on our victim, but my brain has effectively shut down. I mindlessly take a sip of my now cold tea that Rita gave me earlier. With a long sigh, I slowly type out the victim's name.

Davit. Petrosyan.

Enter.

I lay my head on my arms on top of my desk while waiting for the computer to finish its search. The office is eerily quiet—after all, it is barely five a.m. My mind floats back to my dad being laid up in his hospital bed and him yelling at me for a seemingly innocent question before flitting briefly over the interactions I had with two incredibly creepy men, one a day before his untimely death. My interaction with the smarmy guy outside the precinct yesterday was definitely out of the ordinary for me and I can only chalk it up to my over exhaustion.

What is going on with me lately? Is it really just being overly tired? Am I losing my mind?

"...son? Jackson?" A gentle hand touches my shoulder and I startle abruptly, spinning around in my chair, almost punching the figure behind me. As I spin around I come face-to-face with Rita, her dark eyes wide with shock. "You good, Delilah?"

Fuck. "Yeah, sorry Rita. I must've fallen asleep."

"Rough few nights?" I nod in response as she jerks her head toward the computer screen. "What have you found out?"

"Not sure. I haven't even looked. I passed out while waiting on the damn thing to load." I look at the computer screen and I can feel my face go white, bile building up the back of my throat. That's the same man from yesterday afternoon. He is decades younger in his photo, but those eyes were just as dark and evil then as they were when I saw them yesterday. This is the same man who caused me to completely freeze in fear. Who swore up and down that he knew me. And he must've at some point, somehow. He knew my name. I mean, he knew the name I had before my parents adopted me, but I don't remember much of anything before they came into my life. All I know is that this man—this now very dead man—terrified me so deeply in a way I can't explain, in a way I never want to experience again.

I turn my attention back to Davit's file. My eyes skim over his dossier noting that he was arrested for solicitation of a prostitute, possession of crack-cocaine with intent to sell, and lewd and lascivious acts on a minor, just like Bradley Chancler. Also when he was in his twenties! What is with these creeps?! I continue to read down his file when my eyes stop at a familiar name: *Darius Jackson.*

Dad was the lead detective on this case too? What the fuck is going on?!

Turning my attention to Rita as she reads over my shoulder, I ask, "Have the medical examiners come back with any information on Chancler?"

"Yeah, it's one of the reasons I came down here." Rita tosses a manila envelope onto the desk and it lands with a soft thud. I flip through the thin stack of computer paper, trying to make sense of what the medical examiner's report.

REPORT OF INVESTIGATION BY COUNTY MEDICAL EXAMINER

DENT. **Bradley William Chancler** RACE W SEX M AGE 63

First Name   Middle Name   Last Name

ESS **753 El Cajon Blvd, El Cajon 92019** M W S D OCCUPATION **Foreman**

OF DEATH: Violent [X]   Casualty [ ]   Suicide [ ]   Suddenly when in apparent health [ ]   Found Dead [X]

In Prison [ ]   Suspicious, unusual or unnatural [ ]   Cremation [ ]

ent Physical descriptors taken off of drivers license

or Vehicle Accident Check One: Driver [ ]   Passenger [ ]   Pedestrian [ ]   Unknown [ ]

ation by ______ Address ______

gating Agency **San Diego County Police**

ption of Body   Clothed [ ]   Unclothed [ ]   Partly Clothed [X]

Eyes brown   Hair brown & grey   Mustache ______   Beard ______

Weight 197   Length 5' 10"   Body Temp. n/a   Date and Time n/a

Pounds   Feet Inches   Fahrenheit

Rigor Yes [X] No [ ]   Lysed [ ]   Liver Color ______ Fixed [X]   Non-Fixed [ ]

al Wounds Fourth degree burns cover
% of the torso; 100% charred marks on
e head. Synthetic fiber melted into the
back of the biceps and back of torso.
ynthetic hair fiber found melted and
entangled on third digit of left hand.

PROBABLE CAUSE OF DEATH	MANNER OF DEATH	DISPOSITION OF CASE
	(check one only)	1. Not a medical examiner case [ ]
	Accident [ ] Natural [ ]	2. Autopsy requested Yes [ ] No [ ]
	Suicide [ ] Unknown [ ]	Autopsy ordered Yes [ ] No [ ]
	Homicide [X] Pending [ ]	Pathologist ______

by declare that after receiving notice of the death described herein I took charge of the body and made inquiries
ing the cause of death in accordance with Section 21-830-33-030) Massachusetts Code Annotated and that the
ation contained herein regarding such death is true and correct to the best of my knowledge and belief.

Date ______   Place of Investigation ______   Signature of County Medical Examiner ______

"They found a hair melted around his finger but no other evidence?" I tilt my head at Rita before turning back to the line that stood out and yet didn't make any sense whatsoever.

One dark single strand of hair, synthetic in origin.

"A wig hair," she responds as if reading my mind.

CHAPTER EIGHT

After work, I make a trip to the hospital to see my dad. The drive itself is relatively uneventful, and I honestly don't even really remember it. I am surprised that I didn't cause an accident with how drained I am, both mentally and physically. I draw in a deep breath before getting out of the car. I hate having to come to the hospital to see my dad instead of going to see him at my childhood home. Although, I'm not sure what I'm complaining about. I have the freedom to go back to my tiny apartment while Dad is the one stuck hooked up to tubes and wires, struggling to survive. I feel so self-centered in my thinking, but it's mostly just wanting to get back to a sense of normal. But nothing is normal about Dad having cancer, the string of murders rocking our sunny city, the constant screaming coming from my next-door neighbor's apartment, or my sudden adverse reactions to strangers.

Strangers that have both wound up dead.

Ding!

The elevator opens to Dad's floor and it's just as eerily quiet as it was the other day when I came to visit. I silence my phone as I make my way down the hallway, nodding to the staff at the nurses' station as I go. Despite the hallways always smelling like bleach and chlorhexidine, the floor tiles always seem to have a dingy, yellow hue to them. The walls are painted a sterile white and today their starkness makes it feel like they're closing in on me. Red oak wood and muted yellow floors—the color scheme that will forever be ingrained in my brain as the backdrop to the worst moments of my life. First, the death of my mom, and now, watching my dad slowly wither away.

Nurses and doctors pass by with a sense of purpose, their preoccupied, serious expressions reflecting the urgency and dedication that comes with their profession. I catch snippets of their conversations discussing patients and treatment plans, and I'm reminded that this is a place of healing and hope. Even if my brain has associated it with tragedy, there's always a chance, and I know my dad's care team is doing everything they can to help him.

I reach Dad's door and with a heavy sigh, I knock a little louder than I intend to. "Daddy? Can I come in?"

I poke my head around the door frame and I am met with the familiar, steady beep of heart monitors. I push the bulky door open, and its hinges let out a slight creak. After I slip through the tiny gap, it shuts with a loud thud behind me, causing me to flinch as the sound reverberates off the walls. I hate how heavy the doors to the patient rooms are here. You'd think they'd take that into account when constructing a building in which the ill people occupying it will need rest, but I guess not. I quietly pad across the room and cautiously pull back the bleak, papery curtain. Dad's normally dark skin is now ashen and clammy. His breathing is shallow, the rise and fall of his chest nearly imperceptible. My brain begins to think the worst when Dad doesn't respond to any of my calls.

"Daddy? Daddy, are you awake?!" I peer at the frail man's face, his eyes open but glazed, drool hanging out of the corner of his mouth. Panic begins to set in. *No. No. No. No. No. No.* I grab him by the shoulders and start to shake him. "Daddy?! Daddy, wake up! Daddy!"

He startles with a snort, clearly dazed and confused. "Wha...wha...? Who's there?!"

Oh thank the Gods. "Daddy, it's me, Delilah."

He blinks a few times, clearing the sleepiness from his eyes. "Who...who are you?"

"Delilah, Daddy. Your daughter?" I unintentionally add a questioning inflection to the last two words. Surely dementia isn't setting in on top of everything else he is dealing with.

"Hi, honey. Are you okay?" He speaks so clearly, as if he didn't just forget who I was a split second ago.

I lean down and hug him tightly. "I thought you *died*! You were so still!"

He laughs lightly. "You can't get rid of your old man that easily!" He looks me over as I pull back, stray blond tendrils falling into my face. "You look *unwell*, Delilah."

Unwell. Code word for, "you haven't been eating again."

I roll my eyes at the statement. This again. I really don't want to get into this argument right now. Not when there are more pressing matters at hand. It's just easier to blame being overworked for my slowly deteriorating appearance.

"I'm okay, Daddy. Just super busy at work, that's all." It's not a lie. It's just not the whole truth either.

"Uh huh...why don't you tell me what's *really* going on?"

I sigh, looking around at all the "homey" touches we've added around his bed. Pictures of him and Mom in their heyday. The first picture we ever took as a family right after the judge signed the adoption papers. My class graduation picture from the police academy. Dad sees them as his motivation to keep going, to keep pushing and to fight the cancer. All I see are memories of a man that once was.

When did I become so cynical? Is this the early stages of grief?

I dwell on Dad's question a bit more, not entirely sure where to begin. I tried asking him just the other day about his connection to the Bradley Chancler case and he lost his ever-loving mind on me. How exactly am I supposed to talk to him about this if I'm worried he's just going to scream at me again? And how is he even going to react when I tell him that the next victim used my *dead name* even though I don't know this man, and he ALSO has a connection to my Dad?! Realistically, I just need to suck it up, be an adult, and get right to it. I have no problem interrogating witnesses and suspects; surely my Dad, being an ex-detective himself, would and *should* be easier to talk to.

Instead, I decide to start with a topic that's a little easier to broach: my neighbors' constant screaming.

"I keep hearing my next-door neighbors constantly fighting. There's a little girl's voice mixed in among the adults screaming. It's as if no one else hears them! Or they're just ignoring them. And it's always in the middle of the night too! And then the shit at work...It's been too much. I'm just so exhausted."

"Maybe if you ate something, you wouldn't be so tired all the time."

I roll my eyes again. My eating and exercise habits have been a never-ending battle with my parents since I was a kid. Nothing I said ever changed the subject and we would generally get into heated arguments over my caloric consumption. But right now, I have urgent questions that only my dad has the answers to.

"Not sure what that has to do with my bickering neighbors, but okay, Dad." I sigh in resigned exasperation.

We sit in an awkward silence, the soft hum of daytime TV filling the room. I can already feel the bond between my Dad and I shifting. I know as soon as these words leave my mouth, our whole world is going to shatter, but I have to do it. "Why won't you talk to me about your involvement in the Bradley Chancler case from decades ago?"

"I told you the other day, Delilah, to drop it." His eyes narrow.

"And I've told you my entire adult life to stop bringing my eating habits into arguments where they don't belong," I retort, so completely over his way of avoiding topics that make him uncomfortable.

"Delilah..." he growls a warning.

"Dad, this is important! You were the lead detective when Chancler was arrested all those years ago and now he's dead!"

"Good! He deserved to fucking die all those years ago! Prison was too good for that bastard!"

I stare at my dad in shock. I have never heard my Dad speak about any of his prior cases like this before. There is so much anger in his voice, such malice.

Shaking my head to regain composure, I continue, "Okay, but he's dead *now* and I had an interaction with him the day before he died and I don't know why but my gut has been telling me there's something important about this man! And now yet *another* man from one of your cases is dead and he knew my dead name! *And* I ran into him the day before he was murdered, too! *What is going on?! What is the connection?!*"

Dad's face falls. He looks both mortified and sick to his stomach. "Who—who was it?"

"Davit Petrosyan." I sink into my seat as if the weight of the world rests on my shoulders from this answer alone.

"Get off of this case *now*, Delilah! I mean it."

"Absolutely not. What is going on? How do these men know me?!" I slam my hands onto the arm rests in anger and fight hard to keep the unnerving fear out of my voice. Dad has never told me to not take a case, nor has he ever refused to speak about them if I asked.

"You don't need to worry about it. Just tell your captain you can't work on this case anymore." His voice is getting louder and I can't tell if it's out of anger, fear, or both.

I take a deep breath, trying to keep myself from seeing red. I close my eyes to try to maintain my cool and speak through gritted teeth. "What are you not telling me?"

"Drop it, Delilah! For your own good!" he hollers, his voice hoarse.

"I'm not a little kid anymore, Dad! What the fuck is going on!? WHY DO THESE PEOPLE KNOW ME?!" I scream, completely losing my composure as anger floods through me. I'm thirty-five years old, for God's sake! I'm not a child anymore and I am getting so tired of him constantly treating me like one. "This is my *job*! And if you won't give me even *one* iota of information, I'll still press on and figure this out without your help!"

"Delilah Rose, I said—" Dad starts to raise his voice, but before he can finish his sentence, he begins to cough uncontrollably. Any ounce of anger and aggression suddenly dissipates at the sight of him struggling.

"Daddy? Are you—" Without warning, my dad starts coughing up blood before heading into a seizure. "Oh my God!"

I run to the door of his room, yanking it open, hollering for a nurse at the top of my lungs as Dad's heart monitor machine starts to flat line. I am all but thrown out of the room as five nurses run in and the door slams in my face.

Panic-stricken, I stare at the wooden door, trying to see through the little window, but all I see are the bodies of all the nurses moving together like a well-oiled machine around my dad's bed. I begin to shake uncontrollably, backing up until my back hits the wall across from his room. I slide down the wall, sinking onto the floor in a fit of tears.

No. Gods, no. This can't be the end. *Please, someone, please!* Save my Daddy.

CHAPTER NINE

"**M**iss Jackson?"

By the time I am approached by Dad's nurse, it is nearing dinnertime and I can feel the deep red marks that are presumably on my forehead from where my palms were pressed into it and indents of my elbows on my thighs from the pressure. My cheeks and nose are flushed and my eyes swollen from constantly crying. I've known for a few months that Dad was getting worse and I have been trying to mentally prepare myself for the inevitable end, but I'm not quite ready to be hit with the possibility that it could be *now*.

I jump up to my feet, swaying as I move on my legs that have fallen asleep. "Yes?!"

"Your dad is fine, but he's still very weak. He had a tonic-clonic seizure and we had to intubate him, but he's stable for now."

I cross my arms over my chest, rubbing my biceps in a self-soothing motion. "What could've caused him to start seizing? As far as I've heard, he hasn't had one this bad since he was originally hospitalized three months ago."

"We can't say for certain. All of his blood work came back okay so it could be anything, really. Even just the stress of being here and trying to handle chemo treatments," the dark haired man says.

Or the stress from your daughter interrogating you as if you were a murder suspect, I think bitterly. I start to retreat into myself as the self-deprecating thoughts take hold of my brain. What if I'm the reason Dad never recovers? What if I'm the reason Dad gets *worse* because I just can't shut the fuck up and stop questioning him after he told me to drop it?! What if…

No. I can't continue this line of thinking. Not now while Dad is lying in the faded hospital bed with his paper thin sheets fighting for his life. Not now while there's a murderer on the loose in our bustling town and the only connection we've found so far is my dad.

Not. Now.

"Miss Jackson? Miss Jackson, are you all right?"

I shake the spiraling thoughts from my brain and force my eyes to refocus on the nurse. "Yes. Yes. Sorry, it's been a long few days."

"I can imagine." He seems sympathetic enough. Let's be honest though, nothing compares to the shitstorm that this man has certainly dealt with since COVID began running rampant through the world a few years ago. These nurses don't get enough credit for all they have to deal with and all they do. And here I am complaining, albeit internally, about a couple of days with limited sleep. Gods, when did I become so self-centered? Then again, maybe I'm being too hard on myself. What I've been going through while my dad has been sick is no picnic, either. And sleep *is* so important; a lack of it can legitimately kill a person. Or drive them crazy...

"Am I okay to go see him?" I know I must look awful. The fatigue wears on my face and there is no denying it. The circles under my eyes that are normally only a mildly unsettling beiged-out gray-green color are now a dark and prominent blueish-black against my increasingly pallid skin. My lips crack from dehydration, and I have long since chewed off my fingernails.

"You can go in quickly to see him, but he should rest. We'll be running some more tests to make sure all his blood levels are staying stable. We can give you a call with the results if you'd like."

"That would be fantastic. Thank you."

The nurse ushers me back down the hallway to Dad's room, his light-blue scrub pants making a distinct *whooshing* sound as we walk in silence. He gestures to my dad's door and mentions something about a time limit, but he sounds like he's underwater. All the blood rushes to my ears as I struggle not to think about the last time I saw my mother. Her beautiful red hair splayed around her as she laid in the hospital bed. Her normally porcelain-smooth skin peppered with various degrees of abrasions and bruising that had started to blacken. I remember my last image of her well. Seeing my whole world, my savior, my best friend, dying from a careless drunk driver left an indescribable wound in my impressionable sixteen-year-old brain, one that I have never recovered from.

And now, I'm having to face my dad—an intubation tube down his throat, a cannula placed gingerly under his nose, and too many wires and tubes to know where one stops and the other begins.

If he doesn't pull through, I don't think I'll survive it.

Softly, I kiss my father's forehead, keeping my lips pressed against his paling skin. I whisper words of a prayer, or maybe a plea, to the Gods or the Universe or whatever higher power might be out there to keep my daddy safe and alive. I may be in my mid-thirties, but I will always be a daddy's girl, and while my world shattered when my Mom died, I know for certain it will end if I lose my dad too.

A throat clearing sound comes from behind me and Dan, the nurse, is in the doorway, years of dealing with people during the pandemic wearing on his otherwise youthful face. "You should go home and rest. We will call you if anything changes."

I nod in hesitant agreement, whisper "I love you" into the top of my dad's balding head, and make the agonizing trek back to my car.

I plop face down into my bed, not even bothering to undress out of my work suit. The events of the last seventy-two hours weigh heavily on me—my neighbor's constant screaming, the gruesome double homicide case where both victims were somehow connected to Dad, Dad having a violent seizure...This is starting to sound like the stuff of nightmares or a horror movie. I pride myself on being stronger than this. There's not much that I've dealt with after losing my mom that has bothered me, but everything over the last couple of days is wearing down my resolve and I know if I bring this up to anyone at work, I'll be benched due to "mental health concerns." They already think I'm unstable due to my locking compulsion. I don't need to add more fuel to the fire. The only saving grace is that I am a damn good detective and have handled all of my cases with precision and grace. This is probably the only reason they haven't benched me or sent me on paid medical leave.

As I lie in bed, the night surrounds me with its heavy embrace. Restlessness fills my mind, and my body seems to echo the turbulence within. I toss and turn, trying to find a comfortable position, but each shift only seems to heighten my agitation. The softness of the mattress becomes a battleground as I wrestle with my thoughts and emotions from the last few days. I pull the blankets up to my chin, then kick them off again, hoping that changing my body's temperature will somehow ease my jitters. With each twist and turn, the sheets rustle beneath me, creating a gentle cacophony of sounds that seems louder than it actually is. The moonlight filters through the curtains, casting shifting shadows across the room. Their dance against the walls plays tricks on my mind, stepping in time to the rhythm of my inner turmoil.

I try to clear my mind, focus on my breathing, and find the elusive pathway to sleep. But as the minutes turn into hours, it becomes clear that sleep will remain a distant dream for me tonight.

I let out an exasperated sigh of defeat as I surrender to the insomnia. Forcing myself to sit up, I lean against my head board and rub my eyes in an attempt to chase away the exhaustion that seems to envelope me like a heavy cloak. Lifting the phone to check the time, the bright numbers silently taunt me for my futile efforts to find the sandman With a sigh of resignation, I swing my legs over the edge of the bed and plant my feet on the floor. The cold sensation on my skin shocks me awake, momentarily grounding me in the present. I'm giving up on sleep, at least for now. Perhaps a change of scenery will help settle the chaos in my mind.

I begin to pace around my apartment, my skin crawling from an anxiety I can't place. I have no business being this much of a mess and yet, here I am. My skin prickles and the sudden urge to check all the locks overtakes me. I start with the lock on my bedroom window, securing it with the appropriate number of unlock-lock sequences, followed by the living room window. The same routine as always. The same comforting routine that makes me feel secure in my home. As I make my way toward the front door, my blood runs cold and I double over, covering my ears as screams from the little girl next door echo throughout my apartment.

Daddy, no! Please! I don't want to! Please, Daddy, it hurts! NOOOOOOOO!

Every inch of my skin is awash in an icy chill. The screaming continues, reverberating off my tiny apartment walls. How can no one hear this little girl crying out for help? Why isn't anyone stopping this?! I should put a call into 911 that I need back up, but at the rate this little girl is screaming, it could be too late by the time anyone gets here.

I know what I have to do.

I grab my weapon holding onto it tightly as I yank the door open to my apartment, a heated rush of air smacking me in the face. My police training takes over as I barge out of my apartment door into the stale night air. Even though it is only a few feet from my own, the neighbors' door feels like it is a million miles away. I can hear my feet pounding against the concrete floor in my ears. A lump forms in my throat and my body begins to quake as the screaming child gets louder and louder.

How is no one hearing this?!

I pound as loud as I can onto the neighboring door. "Police! Open up!" I scream.

I keep hammering on the door, getting progressively louder with my thumps against the metal and my voice echoing into the empty courtyard below. Soon there are sleepy-eyed residents poking their heads out to watch the commotion I am causing in our otherwise calm complex.

Daddy, please! Please, stop it, Daddy! Momma, help me! Pleeeeeease!

The little girl's terrified voice rings through my ears so loudly that I don't know what else to do but to begin kicking as hard as I can to get it to open. By now, a larger crowd has drawn into the hallway as I land one more final kick that breaks the door open.

"Everybody, freeze! This is the po..." I stare into the dark and empty space in front of me. The apartment is empty.

What the *fuck*?

I slowly close the door, embarrassed and confused. The force of my kicks has made it impossible for the door to sit appropriately in the door frame. What ᴀis going on with me? I'll have a lot of explaining to do to the apartment manager in the morning. Not to mention a hefty fee to replace the door I broke. I can hear the whispers of the neighbors and feel their eyes boring into me as I rush back into my apartment, locking it quickly behind me.

Lock.

Unlock.

Lock.

Unlock.

Lock.

I sink to the floor, my back against the door, gripping my hands into my hair. What is wrong with me?! Am I losing my mind? And why did something about the locking sequence feel...*off*?

I begin to stir as the sun starts filling my apartment. I must have fallen asleep at some point against my own door after the fiasco in the middle of the night. My muscles ache and I feel like I have just run a marathon...barefoot...across Legos. I stretch my legs to reduce any stiffness from sleeping in such an awkward position, even if it was probably only for an hour or two.

I'm so glad to be off today. I'm not entirely sure if I would be able to handle the workload of the last few homicides, plus whatever else might pop up on the radar.

Oh. And can't forget Dad being in the state he's in.

Gods, when did I suddenly lose a complete grip on my life? I should probably get into therapy before anything worse happens. Gods forbid I'm not enrolled if Dad doesn't recover. I would probably lose myself in grief forever, which would then take its toll on my abilities as a detective. I'd probably lose my apartment and become homeless. Maybe Jericho would show me all the safe spots to live out my shattered days. I am suddenly drawn out of my trance of self-deprecating thoughts by my phone vibrating.

Office Management flashes across my screen.

Oh joy.

I sigh heavily and answer with a soft, "Hello?"

"Hi, good morning, Miss Jackson. This is Anne from the leasing office. Are you home by chance? We had some neighbors bring to our attention the damage you did to apartment 218 last night." She sounds almost as if she is asking a question, or maybe being accusatory. In either case, she's not wrong.

There is no use in denying the damages. Besides the *numerous* neighbors that saw me Spartan-kick the door, I'm sure there are cameras lining the courtyard that will easily call my bluff. But how do I explain to my leasing office that I kicked it down because I heard a little girl screaming for help? A sound no one else seemed to hear. And *then* explain the absolute horror I felt when I was met with an empty apartment? If the guys down at the station hear about this, it will definitely put me on desk duty for the remainder of my career. If I don't get shitcanned for this mess I just created for the department. I draw in a deep breath and try to sound as apologetic as possible.

"Good morning, Anne. Yeah, that, uh, that was me," I say sheepishly. "I take full responsibility and will pay for any repairs that need to be done to the apartment."

She seems taken aback by my quick admittance and my offer to pay for the damages. "Workers will be out there later this afternoon to assess the damages and I will send you the invoice," Anne says matter-of-factly. I can just imagine her with her head hung, pressing her thumb and index finger to the bridge of her nose. "I just have to ask, Miss Jackson, *why* did you kick the door down?!"

I let out a nervous laugh, as if that completely absolves me from what I did last night. I figured this question was going to come and honesty is the best policy, right?

"For the last few nights, I've been hearing the neighbors in a screaming match. Last night it seemed to have escalated and then their little girl was screaming for help. It was really loud, and she was screaming for her dad to stop whatever he was doing. I'm a police detective, so I have to intervene when there's imminent danger. Only..." I trail off.

"Only the apartment was empty," Anne says curtly.

"Yeah. That." I suddenly sound like a child being scolded. "I must be overly tired from work lately." Not that that's an excuse, but it's also not much of a lie either. I'm just hoping that it offers some sort of explanation. Or maybe I'm looking for sympathy, even though I don't really deserve it.

"A part of the job, I bet." Anne's voice sounds slightly sympathetic and I hear the slight clicking of a keyboard in the background. A few moments of silence pass and eventually the clicking of the keys stop before her voice picks back up. "I will get you that invoice as soon as the repair men have inspected the damage."

"Okay. Sounds good. Thank you, Anne."

"You're welcome, Miss Jackson. And Miss Jackson?" She pauses and I grunt in acknowledgement. "Please try to get some rest."

Yeah, rest. "Will do. Thank you."

I toss my phone on the kitchen counter, the device skittering slightly across the off-white countertop. I check all the locks again and change into some running clothes. Maybe some fresh summer air will help clear my mind and I can take a nice long nap afterward. After lacing up my shoes, I connect my earbuds to my phone before shoving them in my ears and pocket respectively. I check my window locks a final time before stepping out into the corridor and repeating the proper lock sequence on my door. Walking down the stairs to the communal courtyard, I am met with various side-eyes and neighbors giving me a wide berth as if I were infectious. To avoid more unwanted attention, I pretend to stretch by the gate until the area is clear, then check the lock three times before going for a run.

Why does three locking cycles seem off?

An hour into my run and the San Diego sun has kissed my normally pale skin a light pink. The late summer heat drenches my black tank top and sweat cascades down my forehead and into my eyes. I round the corner and see two well-built men leaning against the archway of my apartment complex. I slow my pace, hoping the two men will move or leave, but their eyes meet mine and I feel a sudden drop in my stomach. My eyes dart between the towering men and the door to my sanctuary. An unreasonable amount of panic sets in as I try to find a way into my building without engaging with these men.

Get it together, Delilah. You're a thirty-five-year-old homicide detective for Gods sake! Stop acting like such a coward! My pep talk doesn't seem to work and the fear must be written all over my face because the men graciously step out of the doorway to allow me entrance into my sanctuary.

That is, until they give my body a complete once over.

They look at each other and smile shit-eating grins before turning back toward me and advancing in my direction. A lump forms in my throat and time seems to stand still as these strangers begin to invade my space. My desire to turn and run as hard and as fast as I can in the opposite direction becomes too prominent to ignore. Except, my body remains rooted in its current spot. As they inch closer, an unspoken conversation happens between the two men and their sly smiles make my skin crawl.

"Delilah!" says the brunette, stretching the last syllable of my name. "Who would've thought we would ever run into you again?"

My heart stops. I don't recognize these men from anywhere and yet, here I am again with more random, seemingly unsavory men saying they recognize me! And, similar to my interaction with Davit Petrosyan, these strangers saying that we've met before is causing every fight-or-flight reaction to take hold of me. I can feel my chest begin to tighten and all I want to do is escape by any means necessary. To run as far away from them as I can as quickly as I can, to melt into the sidewalk and form an indescribable puddle or just disappear completely from existence. Anything that would make me invisible to the gaze of these men. Unfortunately, I can't seem to move. I can't even breathe! I feel like a small child caught in the act of stealing a cookie from the cookie jar with the thought process of "if I don't move, they can't see me."

Except there is no cookie. There is no jar. And I am not a child.

As if by some fate of the Gods or a miracle, Anne, the apartment manager, opens the gate to our complex interrupting whatever sinister transaction was transpiring between the two men.

"Mr. Bancroft! Mr. Duggard! Thank you for coming in early. We had a minor problem with the unit we originally had reserved for you." I can feel Anne shift her eyes over to me disapprovingly before turning back to the guests and plastering a beaming smile on her face. "But we were able to find a similar unit that I think would be perfect for you." Her voice trails off as she ushers the two men into the gated courtyard.

The moment they are out of my sight, a wave of relief washes over me. I bend over, placing my hands on my knees, willing myself to breathe and slow my racing heart. I don't know what has gotten into me, but I'm not sure how much more of this I can take. I decide to continue on for another run in hopes that I will be able to force myself into an exhaustive sleep before work tomorrow. A sleep that will drown out all of the nightmares, both fictional and those that have been haunting me in the waking world.

CHAPTER TEN

*T*hree a.m.

Up before my alarm, as per usual, but sleep, for once, did not run from me. I feel slightly more well-rested than I have the previous nights. From the sheer exhaustion of running from my problems yesterday, I ended up passing out in my bed still fully clothed in my running gear. A decision I now fully regret. My body is still warm and sticky from the intense, panic-induced workout out in the blazing heat of the summer sun, and my sweat-soaked workout clothes cling uncomfortably to my skin. The air in the room feels stifling, and I kick off the blankets in an attempt to cool down, cursing these damn apartments for only having a window unit for air conditioning. It should be illegal in California to *not* have cooling throughout the whole house. I carefully peel out of my crusty socks and shoes, tossing them into my laundry pile. I will have to make sure I get laundry done today before it stinks up the place. Stripping out of my tank top and leggings is more of a struggle than normal, as the salt of the sweat has practically molded them to my body. My skin feels clammy, and I shiver involuntarily as the cool air brushes against my damp body.

I cross into my bathroom, cautious to avoid looking at my scarred body in the mirror. Self-image issues are nothing new to me, but seeing the visual reminders of a past before my mom and dad saved me sometimes just makes me feel worse about a situation I can't remember. Today is one of those days. Sometimes I wonder if it's a good thing that I have completely blocked out whatever life I had prior to my parents adopting me. Other times, I wonder if it's something I should look into. Maybe it would bring clarity to all the areas of my life that seem to be so muddy.

Like this damn locking sequence that now feels completely off.

But also *right?*

Or maybe it would help explain the visceral reactions I've been having lately to certain interactions with strangers. The worst part of it is that it's not *all* strangers, which, while that would be frustrating, at least then I'd be able to predict when it's going to happen. But instead, it's only been the last couple of them that I have had the displeasure of running into. The ones that have mysteriously died the next day and that Dad seems to lose all composure over when I bring up their names. It's almost as if my body has never interacted with a stranger before, like I'm some sort of hermit who has never come into contact with off-putting men before. Or something like that. I wish my dad would talk to me more about my past instead of just pushing it aside or changing the subject completely. I honestly think he forgets that I'm not a little girl anymore, but I know he always has my best interests at heart. Right?

As I continue to ponder the events of the last few days, I turn on the shower for a quick wash off and the soothing sound of water hitting the tile fills the air. I step into the stream of hot water, washing away the sweat and grime of the workout. The sensation is refreshing and invigorating, as if the water is purifying both my body and mind. I close my eyes, letting the water run down my face, removing any lingering tension and worries. The weight of the day's stress melts away, replaced by a sense of calm. I scrub my hair and my body clean, feeling a little more human. My muscles still ache from the panicking, minute amount of sleep, and heavy run I did yesterday, but I actually feel *human.*

"Kicking in the non-existent neighbors' door probably didn't help either," I say bitterly out loud to no one.

Sighing heavily, I turn off the shower and wrap my hair in a towel. On my counter I see a light purple bag of Epsom salt that Dad gave me before he ended up in the hospital. *Chronic Pain and Fatigue Body Soak.* The bright yellow sticky note is still attached to it displaying Dad's words of encouragement:

I am proud of you. Just make sure you don't forget to take care of yourself while you take care of others. Love, Dad.

A slight smile crosses my lips. "Okay, Dad. I'll take the hint," I speak into the universe.

I turn the faucet back on and dump a heaping amount of the bath soak into the bottom of the tub in an attempt to wash all my worries away. Not that I really think that a hot soak in some expensive salt and essential oils is going to solve all of my problems, but it's a nice Band-Aid for the shitstorm that has become my every waking moment the last few months.

Carefully, I step into the tub, feeling the warmth embrace my feet, easing tired muscles that I didn't even realize hurt. I settle into the water, allowing it to envelop me in a cocoon of comfort. A sigh of relief escapes my lips as the warmth settles into my skin, the sensation nearly turning my bones to jelly. Steam rises off the water, the smell of blueberries and citrus wafting into my nose.

"Alexa," I say loud enough for the device to hear me. "Play relaxing forest sounds."

She dings in acknowledgement and the music of nature fills my tiny bathroom. In this moment, the world outside ceases to exist. There is only the soothing sensation of the water, the comforting warmth seeping into my pores, and a profound sense of calm. The weight of responsibilities and worries dissolve around me for the first time in a long while. If this is what Dad meant by "take care of yourself," I should do this more often. I can feel my eyelids growing heavier the more I relax and, for once, I ignore all of my instincts to jump out of the bath and into the safety of my blankets.

TRIGGER WARNING

Please be warned that this chapter is probably one of the darkest chapters in The Fifth Lock. Read with caution. This chapter consists of child abuse (on page fade to black and off page), child sexual exploitation (off page), and child rape (off page).

If this chapter triggers any sort of strong emotion, please seek help from your counselor or trusted confidant.

Remember; this is just a story. But for some, it may be their real life. If you or anyone you know needs help, please use the resources listed below and at the beginning of this book to seek help or more information.

Stay safe and mind your mental health. It is important. YOU are important.

MISSING CHILD AND ABUSE HOTLINE: 800-843-5678
MISSING AND EXPLOITED CHILDREN HOTLINE: 800-222-3463
HUMAN TRAFFICKING HOTLINE: 888-373-7888

CHAPTER ELEVEN

From the outside, the yellow stucco house on Chateau Drive resembles any other house in this sunny, suburban neighborhood. With its perfectly manicured lawn and high wooden fencing that guards the backyard, you would never suspect that the inside of this single family home hides a dark secret behind its walls. Curtains are consistently drawn shut on the windows to hide the horrors that take place inside.

Inside the home, the walls, once painted in vibrant colors, are now faded, cracking and chipped in most places, revealing the rough plaster underneath. Patches of mold and mildew cling to every corner, showcasing the minimal care and effort the homeowners have put into the house. Dull, dusty couches, mismatched chairs, and numerous piles of dust bunnies litter the sparsely decorated living room. Unidentifiable stains discolor various parts of the hardwood floors and the fabric of the couches. Mountains of pet hair take up every corner space while a bowl of untouched, molding pet food sits in the kitchen, its recipient long since missing. Lines of white powder streak the coffee table, the only clean surface in the house. An emaciated woman is slouched lifelessly on the couch, drool pooling at the corners of her mouth, with a tourniquet around her arm and a hypodermic needle dangling out of the crook of her elbow.

Pacing in front of the drug-induced woman are three men in the middle of a heated argument. The first man, tall and imposing, gestures emphatically as he speaks, his voice commanding attention. His brows furrow and he leans forward, as if trying to incite fear in the older, thin man.

"Where is she?! You promised her to us!" The man's voice echoes throughout the otherwise empty home.

The second man, with a more measured demeanor, paces back and forth, his arms crossed in front of his chest. His eyes blaze with conviction as he too awaits an answer from the man of the house. Agitation is written clear as day on his face.

"She's around here somewhere. Little slut couldn't have gone far!" the thin older man answers, words slurring. His cheeks are sunken in and a patchy five o'clock shadow weathers his face.

Their voices continue to reverberate off the walls, creating an almost overwhelming cacophony. The furniture itself seems to shrink away, as if trying to distance itself from the verbal onslaught. As the argument escalates, the men's body language becomes more assertive, their postures tense, and their gestures begin bordering on the aggressive. There are no physical altercations, but the energy in the room is charged with the potential for an explosive conflict. The woman on the couch is unfazed by the scene that is playing out in front of her, either from having grown accustomed to this type of interaction over time or the drugs coursing through her veins or both.

As the argument reaches its peak, there is a moment of collective silence, a moment where all three men catch their breath and lock eyes. The weight of the disagreement hangs heavily in the air. Whatever the younger two men were hoping to accomplish is not going as they had planned, and their patience seems to be wearing thin at the excuses that the older one gives.

"She better be ready when we come back at five or the deal is off! As it is, Tyler," the younger of the three men sneers, yanking the door open, the cool air bursting into the space. "She's not even worth the five grand you asked! She's USED goods. You'll be lucky if I give you two! And don't forget that little bitch *bit* me." The man spits his words like venom before slamming the front door shut, shaking the walls.

A few minutes tick by and the anger in the homeowner begins to boil as he stares at the closed door in front of him.

"CHILD!" he shrieks at the top of his lungs, his face red-hot with anger. His outburst causes the woman on the couch to jump for a split second before she smacks her lips and sinks deeper into the couch.

Heavy footsteps stomp along the creaky hardwood floor, his aggression permeating the dilapidated room. The smell of urine, feces, and sex fills the air. Yellow stains from cigarette smoke stain the walls, adding to the myriad of atrocious smells that leech into every surface of the home. Lines of ants march to and fro across the walls to destinations unknown. Cockroaches skitter around the angry man's feet as he pounds down the hallway. This is a house that should have been condemned ages ago.

Hidden in the closet with clothes too small for even a tiny frame such as hers, a young girl no older than nine presses herself as far into the corner as possible, trying to keep herself concealed. Her wide eyes dart around the darkened space, searching for any sign of safety, anything else she could hide behind. A pile of stuffed animals, random garbage bags, *anything*. The child's heart beats rapidly, echoing in her ears loudly as if she's in front of a drum choir. She squishes herself further against the back wall, hoping to disappear into the shadows as the fuming man's rage reverberates off every vacant wall in her room. She begins to pray that the man who is supposed to protect her gets tired of trying to find her and just gives up. It's not the usual course of events when he's angry, but it's a thought that always runs through her head when he's on a tirade.

Through the slightly ajar door, a sliver of light seeps in, casting eerie shadows on the walls of her hiding place. The child's breath catches with every creak of the floorboards and every rustle of the wind outside. Each sound, however faint, seems like an ominous harbinger of danger. In her hyper-vigilant state, her mind races with frightening scenarios, her imagination conjuring up the worst possibilities. Although, she knows that whatever she dreams up is not nearly as frightening as what actually awaits her once her father finds her. As she continues to cower in the only place she could seek solace in, she yearns for the presence of a caring adult to shield her from the nightmare of a life she has lived during her few short years on this earth. She longs for a reassuring voice, a gentle touch, and the embrace of someone who can make the fear vanish with a single word.

A feeling she has never gotten with either of her parents.

Her teachers seem to ignore her as well, no matter how disheveled her countenance when she comes to school. This always leads to the other kids in her class bullying her for her matted hair or the clothes that don't quite fit. Everyone is always quick to tear down her dirty appearance, but no one ever says a word about the bruises that mar her pale skin.

The girl shrinks further into herself, covering her ears, trying to muffle the sound of doors slamming and items being thrown as Tyler curses and screams for her. Maybe if she stays quiet for long enough, the bad man won't find her. How she hopes and prays that tonight she will get out of his rage-induced assault alive. Maybe he will get distracted and go back to his lines of white powder on the coffee table. Maybe tonight will be the night she musters up the courage to run and try to get help.

Maybe. But probably not. It's the same song and dance in her head through every abusive episode that she will find her strength to run; that she will *finally* be able to use her voice and tell someone, *anyone*, about the atrocities that go on in her house. She is always just one step away from telling a random stranger on the street until Tyler starts to shower her with love and attention, saying things like:

"It'll never happen again. I love you, baby bug."

"You're such an amazing, little, cash cow. My sweet baby bug."

And then he gives her new toys that will only end up broken a few days later during one of his fits of rage. Then the cycle of the young child wanting to run and beg for help starts all over again.

Why don't they love her? Why must every display of affection come with a price? Why can't they just leave her alone? The bruising on her pallid, freckled skin hasn't even had a chance to fade from their last encounter.

The floor creaks outside of her hiding spot and she covers her mouth in an attempt to stifle her panicked breathing. She squeezes her eyes tight, tears rolling down her dirty, gaunt face. Silently she finds herself praying to an unknown deity once again to save her from this hell. To make her father just turn around and not search for her anymore. Not just for the remainder of his aggressive tantrum, but for the rest of his life. For the rest of *her* life. She prays that he will just leave her there to rot because that's better than going through any more of this torture.

The closet door jerks open causing the young girl to recoil from the sudden burst of light.

A clear indication that both of her prayers have gone unanswered, again.

"You!!" the thin man growls. "You cost me money, you fucking whore!"

The girl doesn't say a word. She's not even sure what to say. She knows that no matter what she says, the man will turn it back on her. He always does. She wonders how could this man who is supposed to love and care for her call her such vulgar names, how he can continually sell her off to the next highest bidder to do with her as they please. Doesn't he love her anymore? Did he ever love her? Were the days he called her his "little baby bug" just false memories?

"Nothin' to say fer yerself?!" he sneers. When the child doesn't answer quickly enough, he lurches down and grabs her by her arm, yanking her upward. She tries as hard as she can to stifle the cry of pain as his dirty fingernails dig deep into her bicep. Any sound from her signifying any level of discomfort always makes him even angrier, and she can only imagine the amount of punishment she is going to receive this time. He reeks of cheap vodka and stale cigarettes, powdered remnants of his drug of choice lining his nostrils. Today it is cocaine.

"Quit yer bitchin'!" he spits in her face as he tosses her onto the floor outside of the closet. The small girl's frame hits the hard floor with a loud thud, sending dust everywhere. She bites her lip hard enough to draw blood as she makes a valiant attempt to not make any noise.

The child crawls toward the door in an attempt to get away from her drunk father, his words slurring and his body lumbering. "I'm sorry," she whimpers in a feeble attempt to lessen his anger. No matter how small and meek she tries to make herself, she knows there is no reasoning with him when he gets like this. He doesn't like losing out on money, and this is her third strike this month from callers that have come to stake their claim on her young body.

The first strike was when one of The Bad Men had become enraged that she didn't know how to "properly suck his dick" as instructed. The man blamed the her father for not "teaching her properly." Tyler responded by not feeding her for a week as punishment. He said that she made him look like a fool. The next two weeks after that were a blur of her father forcing himself into her mouth until she "got it right." The second was when a different man attempted to shove his unwashed, lesion-covered penis into her mouth. He had succeeded in getting it in, but when he held her head to "help her along," she bit as hard as she could until the man punched her upside the head, causing her to release him. The punishment from Tyler was much worse than the blow to the head from the foul man

Her father punched her repeatedly in the mouth that night, causing her to lose a few baby teeth in the process. But that wasn't her only punishment. To pay for her insolence, the poor girl was forced to service her father in any manner he chose—sometimes with multiple Johns, sometimes with blunt instruments, and, worse, sometimes with a hot curling iron—for two whole months. She knew this third strike was going to be the death of her. And she wished and prayed for this to be the day that her soul left her body.

"Oooh no." A devilish smile creeps across his face. "You know that shit don't fly, little lady. You've been a bad girl and you know I don't like when you're an insufferable brat!" His words cut like ice. Each insult thrown like a dagger at her. "Maureen!" Tyler bellows. "Bring me the iron!"

The child's eyes widen and well up with tears. "No! No! Please! I'm sorry! I won't do it again!"

He advances on her, grabbing her by the hair and dragging her over to the dingy, stained mattress that lies on the floor. She puts all her energy into struggling against the hold Tyler has on her hair, but with every ounce of resistance, he only grips her tighter. Maureen stumbles into the room, her clothes and hair disheveled, a curling iron attached to an extension cord in one hand, a lit cigarette in the other. The frail girl's eyes bulge as she is tossed backward onto the bed. She makes an attempt to scramble farther back, failing miserably as Tyler latches onto her ankle, pulling her back to him.

"Please! Please! I'll be good! I promise! I'll make the money back for you," the girl wails.

At just nine years old, this small child knows all the ways to beg and plead for her life. To beg and plead to "make things better" in ways no child should have ever learned. Unfortunately, tonight, it doesn't seem like those pleas are going to be the solution.

Maureen, visibly high on who knows what, crawls across the bed, grabbing the girl's wrists and pinning them down. The little girl flails, kicking at the man as he wrestles with her legs to pull down her shorts.

"Daddy, please! Please stop it!" With one misplaced kick, the struggling child lands her foot square across her father's jaw, splitting his lip. At the notice of her blunder, she stills with baited breath waiting for the explosion that is obviously brewing underneath Tyler's twitching forehead vein.

Tyler wipes at his face and notices the splotch of blood on the back of his hand as he pulls it away. With a deep, angry breath, he narrows his eyes at his terrified charge, rears back and backhands the girl, splitting her lip open and causing the start of a black eye.

"If you make the neighbors call the cops on me again, that will be the least of your worries!"

The girl cries uncontrollably, fighting against her fathers' calloused hands as he forces her legs open, pinning them down with his knees.

"Momma, help me! Pleeeeeease!" the child cries frantically, her eyes locked on her father's hand as he brings the hot curling iron right in between her legs.

CHAPTER TWELVE

"Aaaaahhhh!" I wake up screaming at the top of my lungs and thrashing around in the bathtub, water tidal-waving onto the tile floor. I clutch at my chest, willing myself to breathe through an onslaught of tears and unexplained fears. As I push myself into a sitting position, I notice my towel is soaked and falling off of my head. I must've sunk down into the water during my impromptu nap. The bath has turned ice cold, causing my legs to feel like lead and no matter how hard I try, I can't seem to make them move. If this is going to become a common occurrence where I can't move my extremities, I'm going to have to rethink my career choice for the first time in my life.

No. I will not even entertain that thought. Instead, I force myself out of the frigid water, drain the tub and ring my water logged towel out before draping it over the edge of the porcelain to dry. I grab two more towels from under the sink, wrapping my hair in one and the other around my body. Despite the summer heat seeping into the apartment, a chill runs across my skin. A quick check of my phone shows that it's only five in the morning. I'm not due into work until nine, which gives me more than enough time to get a load of laundry done. Towel drying my hair, I pick out black leggings and a t-shirt from my dresser. I strip my bedding and toss it into the hamper along with my sneakers. I plop a book and a can of Sprite Zero on top of the basket along with a small bottle of detergent before heading out the door after my usual locking sequence.

Three locks. Three clicks. Everything about this numerical routine is supposed to promote safety. But why does it also feel so foreign all of a sudden?

Thankfully, there's no one in the laundry room today. I think the pea green walls are supposed to offer some sort of calming effect, but really it just feels like an outdated color choice. Along one wall sits the two coin-operated washers. Both are big enough to fit my entire laundry bag, including my bedding. To the right of them, four miniature dryers are neatly stacked on top of one another, forming a compact tower that seems to defy gravity. To the left of the washers is a battered, stained, standalone farmhouse-style sink. I'm not entirely certain anyone ever even uses it, but the stains seem to imply otherwise. A white metal table—complete with dents, scratches, and various carvings from the teenagers that reside in the complex—sits opposite the washers and dryers with two uncomfortable metal chairs placed haphazardly around it.

The one thing I hate about this apartment is having a communal laundry room, where you always have to be on edge. Sometimes someone will grab your clothes out of the washer and toss them onto the table so that they can use it next, even if the cycle isn't quite done yet. Which, given the constantly filthy state of the table, means that the clothes need to be rewashed. I've had it happen a time or two, so now I just sit in the laundry room and wait it out to make sure clothes don't go missing or don't finish washing properly. After throwing my laundry in, I hop up on the table and open my book, immersing myself in a fantasy land of witches, vampires, and a princess with a curse. Fantasy books have always been my favorite genre. The thrill of magic and adventure—typically complete with a happy ending—just feels like a breath of fresh air in comparison to my daily life and the horror and sadness I see and deal with at work.

Ten minutes into my book, a chill runs down my spine, gooseflesh erupting all over my skin. Panic begins to set in, but I can't seem to find the cause of this reaction. That is, until I look up from my book to find the two men from yesterday, Sean Bancroft and Mike Duggard, entering the laundry room. Their demeanor instantly shifts from a jovial, deep belly laughter to a sneer. My eyes widen as they approach me. My heart pounds faster, its relentless rhythm echoing in my ears. Sweat forms on my forehead, dampening my brow despite the coolness of the room from the loud, outdated, air conditioning wall unit. I desperately seek to find an escape, a sanctuary from whatever intuitive reaction my body keeps having to these strange men. Yet, the heavy weight of their presence holds me rooted in place, a captive to my own fear.

"It's so good to see you again, Delilah," Bancroft drawls. His accent reminds me of someone from the deep south. Definitely not something you would ordinarily hear in Southern California. He is older than the man Anne called Mike, but not by much. His hair is a dark chocolate brown with wisps of gray forming at his temples and dispersing through his clean cut beard. A warm, golden tan graces his skin, reflecting a life spent under the sun's gentle caress. The healthy glow brings out the subtle contours and defined muscles. His tanned complexion speaks of adventures in far-flung destinations or of spending his days lazing about the numerous beaches our state has to offer. Either could be possible. But regardless of how conventionally attractive Sean might be, I keep getting brought back to his greeting the two times we've now met: *it's good to see you again.*

I am certain I have never seen this man in my entire life. Neither he nor Duggard, the dirty blond, lanky man who looks like he just rolled out of bed. But this isn't the only time I have had an encounter like this where mere strangers seem to recognize me, but I don't have a clue as to who the hell they are. I fight back against the quiver I feel in my throat before I speak.

"I'm sorry, but I don't believe I know you." I have faked confidence for my entire career at the precinct, certainly I can do it for these two individuals. If I've learned anything over the years, it is to never let the opposing side know that they have an upper hand in your emotions. Remain calm, cool, collected. Don't let them see your weakness.

Bancroft takes a few steps forward, closing the gap between us. I pretend to not notice and stare down at my book, feigning like I am reading. Anything to signify that I am done with this conversation, anything to distract myself from the knots twisting in my stomach. He is so close I can smell him. He smells of Irish Spring and suntan oil. My stomach lurches in repulsion at the odd mixture of scents. It takes everything I have to not vomit on the spot. Everything inside me is screaming to get away, to run as far as I can, just like the last time I encountered him. But where can I run to? How can I get away? Sean is in my personal space, and his accomplice is leaning against the doorframe of the tiny laundry room.

I am trapped.

Bancroft leans closer, his face inches from mine. I lean back and wrinkle my nose in disgust, a clear indicator of being unappreciative of this strange man being so close to me. He either doesn't notice or doesn't care. His arrogance and lack of general etiquette for a woman's social cues reminds me of Jimmy, which only heightens my disdain for this mystery man.

"You know," he purrs, "now that we're neighbors, we could always continue what we started all those years ago." He puts his muscular forearms on either side of my small frame.

"I'm sorry?" I speak with a questioning inflection. What the hell does he mean "continue what we started"?! Before another word can be spoken, the buzzer to the washing machine rings throughout the room. Bancroft pushes off the table, allowing me to hop down. I can feel his eyes boring into my back as I stride the few feet from where I was sitting over to the washer. I become hyper-aware of my movements, and instead of bending down like I usually would to grab the clothes from the washer, I opt to squat. Trying my hardest to not let his gaze to linger on any one part of my body longer than necessary.

As I start loading the dryer with my wet clothes, the surrounding air begins to feel heavy. Without looking behind me, I can feel both men's presence creeping up on me. The previous, slightly more familiar scent from Bancroft assaults my nose first before being followed up by the overpowering smell of Axe body spray that must be from Mike. I choke on the all-consuming mix of the three competing aromas. As the two older men close in on my personal space once again, a blatant unease engulfs me. I can feel their predatory energy pressing in on me from both sides, invading my carefully guarded boundaries. My heart quickens its pace, beating against my chest like a caged bird, desperate to break free from the tightening grip of discomfort. My senses sharpen as if a switch has been flipped, heightening my perception of the world closing in.

Every fiber of my being tingles with a mix of vulnerability and defensiveness. My muscles tense, ready to respond at a moment's notice, just like I trained for at the academy. But this is the real world, not a controlled environment, and I'm alone—no weapon, no backup. So now, it's all about my primal instincts, my innate desire to protect myself and preserve a sense of autonomy. The sensation of being on edge is suffocating, like an invisible force field has shrunken in around me. The walls seem to inch closer, crowding my thoughts and limiting my freedom of movement. I feel a growing urge to retreat, to create distance between myself and the encroaching bodies, but with the dryers in front of me and the men behind me, I am trapped. In this moment, I am suddenly acutely aware of my own boundaries.

The duality of emotions stir within me, a mix of discomfort, unease, and a hint of vulnerability. Yet, amidst the encroachment, a spark of resilience flickers within. I remind myself of my own agency, my power to assert my boundaries and reclaim control over my own space and my own body. I remind myself that I am a homicide detective, one of the best! I remind myself that I am a Jackson. A family built on strength and consent. I slam the door to the dryer shut and whirl around to confront these assholes, who audaciously decided that *my* personal space was fit for their bodies. My eyes blaze red hot as I summon the strength to assert myself, and I shift in an exaggerated way to create a small but significant gap between myself and the encroachers. It is nothing short of a silent declaration, a not so gentle reminder—more to myself than these cretins—that my space is sacred and deserving of respect.

"Please move," I snarl through gritted teeth.

Duggard rebukes my command and presses his body forward, placing his hand on the dryer next to my head, creating a blockade with his arm. A saccharine smile washes over his face.

"Aww, come on now, baby. Can't you ask a little nicer?" he snickers. "You sound so angry. Nothing like the good little girl I know."

My skin crawls and every survival instinct I have ignites inside me. "I said, move."

Bancroft places himself opposite Duggard, mirroring his body language.

"Aww, it doesn't seem like our little *friend* remembers her manners, Mike," the dark-haired man coos, inching his face closer to my ear. I can feel his hot breath on my neck, the stench of beer and cigarettes assaulting my nostrils. I force myself to remain still, to not show that any part of me is completely in shock and trembling at their closeness. My usual confident demeanor inexplicably disappears around these men, and the cacophony of smells between the two of them isn't helping to eliminate the waves of nausea threatening to make a mess all over their shoes.

Mike Duggard takes his free hand and traces my jaw line, his calloused fingertips feeling like sandpaper against my skin. I jerk my head away and growl, "Don't. Touch. Me."

Both men laugh, moving their bodies to cover mine. I can feel their body heat radiating off of them, and that mixed with the heat from the dryer becomes too much, causing my heart rate to surge and sweat to bead where my hairline meets my neck.

"It seems like our little *pet* forgot how good she can feel." Bancroft's lip curls upward in a sinister smile.

"It seems you're right, Sean. Maybe she needs a reminder," Mike snickers, suddenly shoving his hand between my thighs. In an instant, all of my training on preventing a sexual assault escapes me. My mind blanks. This is it. I am going to lose my sanctuary to some assholes that just moved in. And who would believe me? Me, a cop, who couldn't stop two men from groping her in the laundry room. Silent tears slide down my cheeks as Mike's lips meet my throat, his beard causing friction burns on the sensitive skin there. The world around me fades to black as their hands roam across my exposed skin.

"Delilah?" a gruff, familiar voice perforates the still air bringing me back to reality. Both men stop their assault on my body and turn toward the sound. It takes my eyes a minute or two to refocus and blink through the tears to see Jericho. "Are you okay?"

He sounds like he's underwater. His voice is drowned out by that screaming child that no one else seems to notice. WHY ISN'T ANYONE HELPING HER?!

Mike and Sean push off the dryers. "Still just as ornery, I see. We were just leaving anyway."

They walk toward the veteran, who is shooting daggers from his eyes at them.

"Come see us if you ever want to try again," Mike laughs as he and Sean disappear around the corner.

Mouth agape, I sink to the cold concrete floor. The tears stop, but my body is still trembling. Jericho rushes toward me, his worn out sneakers squeaking against the floor. He swoops down and wraps me in his arms.

"Are you okay?!" he questions, smoothing my hair with one of his hands. His skin has been darkened by the summer sun, but there is something else different about him. I can't place it in this moment, but Jericho feels...*different*.

I don't speak for a few minutes, but he doesn't press the issue. Jericho sits on the cold floor with me in his arms. As I begin to recover from the assault, I finally take a long look at Jericho. His face is washed and clean-shaven. His clothes aren't dirty and ragged. I blink at him a few times.

"You got new clothes!"

Jericho beams his crooked smile. "I did! I finally got help from the VA! They helped me get a job and even helped me get a safe place to stay. So...hey neighbor!"

I stare at him, trying to take in everything he just said. Something in my brain isn't clicking right away, but when it does, I squeal like a child and launch myself at him, wrapping my arms around his neck. "Oh, Jericho! That's fantastic! You're finally getting what you deserve! You know, in a good way. We'll have to go visit Dad and tell him."

Jericho smiles a toothy grin and then frowns. "Hey, D, what was going on when I walked in?"

I cast my eyes downward and start chewing my bottom lip. I don't want to believe what just happened. I don't want to believe that I was assaulted in my own apartment complex. How do I explain that I wasn't strong enough to fight off these two men, but I'm strong enough to do my job as a homicide detective? How do I even explain how those men make me feel, how the things they said struck a chord somewhere deep in my chest, even when they don't make sense to me? I feel like I'm going crazy, with my sleepless nights and phantom neighbors, the nightmare I had in the bathtub—like a dream of someone else's memory—and this case, with all the victims having criminal histories and my father demanding I recuse myself. How can I properly protect the citizens of my city by finding this murderer if I can't even protect myself in my own backyard? Before I have the opportunity to seriously consider this possibility or even ease any worry Jericho might have, the dryer buzzes, and it snaps me out of my downward spiral. I quickly stand up, grabbing my hamper off the metal table.

"I'm so excited that your life is turning around, Jer!" I shut the dryer, avoiding the question that still hangs in the air between us. I lean the basket on my hip and give him a one-armed hug.

"After you get settled, we'll have to have dinner or something! Maybe we can bring some takeout to Dad and eat together. But right now I need to go get ready for work. I'll see you soon!"

He grunts and smiles in response as I run out of the room to my one bedroom apartment—my little sanctuary.

CHAPTER THIRTEEN

I make it back to my apartment without incident and I thank the Gods, because I'm not quite sure what would happen if I ran into Sean or Mike again. My heart finally returns to normal once I am in the safety of my own home. I have never had my personal space invaded like that before and I never want to experience it again. As I go through the motions of finishing my preparations to head to work, my mind starts to replay everything from the last twenty-four hours.

The weight of these memories bears down on my heart, leaving me feeling more lost and broken than I have in years. It's as if the world has shifted, and everything I once knew has been shattered into pieces. I replay the scenes in my mind, each one more haunting than the last. The images are chiseled into my consciousness, and I can't escape them.

Dad coughing up blood and seizing.

Hearing a girl screaming for help in an apartment that turned out to be empty.

A very vivid and horrific nightmare of a young girl being abused.

And now an assault from two grown men who reside in my complex.

I find myself asking why. Why are all of these traumatizing events happening to me?! And one right after the other! I take a deep breath. While there doesn't seem to be any correlation between all the events that have been happening and anything from my past that I can remember, there must be something, and I intend to find out what it is. I finish packing my gym bag and changing into a pair of black slacks and a blouse. I check my reflection in the mirror of the bathroom one last time and cringe.

There, I see an image that tells the story of my recent exhaustion and weariness. My blue eyes, usually bright and vibrant, now appear dull and heavy, burdened by weeks of fatigue. The circles under them have definitely darkened over the last few days, evidence of all the sleepless nights, restless thoughts, and stressful work situations I've been experiencing.

My pale skin is lackluster and is tinging on gray. Lines of fatigue have carved their way around my eyes and mouth, revealing the toll that stress and exhaustion have taken on my once-youthful appearance. My cheekbones are more pronounced and it seems like I've lost more weight in the last few days than I have over the last few months, though I'm sure it's just an illusion. My shoulders sag, and I can see the weight of the world resting heavily on them. The lines of worry and tension in my forehead seem to have taken up permanent residence, reminding me of the constant strain I've been under.

As I gaze at myself in the mirror, I see a person who has been running on empty for far too long. The demands of life, both physical and emotional, have left me feeling drained and depleted. There's a weariness in my eyes that seems to reach deep into my soul. It's as if the energy that once fueled my spirit has been sapped, leaving me feeling like a flickering flame on the verge of burning out.

My curly hair, usually neat and well-kept, is now disheveled and a rats nest of varying shades of blond. I haven't had the energy or motivation to care for my appearance as I once did. I manage to rake my fingers through it, detangling it slightly, and pull it back into a low, messy ponytail. I purse my lips at the sight of myself in the mirror, a longing for the rest and rejuvenation I so desperately need washing over me. After all of this—whatever this is—is over, I need a vacation.

And a long nap.

As I turn away from the mirror, I resolve to make a change. I will seek moments of rest, find solace in simple joys, and take the time to care for myself. I know this is what Dad would want for me.

I sigh as I swing my bag over my shoulder and walk out my door into the blinding early morning sun. As the door opens, I'm greeted by a burst of vibrant colors. Sunlight dapples the terracotta flooring of the tranquil courtyard, the short palm trees providing shade across the open space here and there. The sky overhead is clear and endless, and the warmth of the sun envelops me as I step out into the hallway, pulling the door closed behind me. I take a deep breath, savoring the sweetness of the summer air. After fiddling with my lock in the manner that makes me feel safe, I make my trek down to the parking garage, leaving the memories of the last few hours behind me.

I walk into the precinct and I am instantly hit with a sense of something not being right. I can sense a palpable shift in the atmosphere. Conversations hush and I become acutely aware of my own presence, feeling like an outsider in a space that once felt welcoming. Each step feels heavy, and I become hyper-aware of every move I make, trying not to impose myself on others.I try to smile and engage with those around me, hoping to break the invisible barrier that has seemingly sprung up. However, my attempts are met with fleeting glances and awkward silences, as if everyone is purposefully avoiding me. I reach the locker room and Rita and I lock eyes. I watch as the color drains from her bronze face and she spins around trying to avoid having any conversation with me.

"Hey, Rita!" I holler out. Rita freezes in her tracks and I watch her entire body stiffen. In that moment, I feel a mix of emotions wash over me. Confusion clouds my mind as I search for any clues or reasons behind this sudden alienation. My heart aches with a tinge of sadness, wondering if I unintentionally did something to upset or offend those around me. Did my OCD finally get to Rita too?

"What is going on with everyone today? Who died?" I try to jest.

Rita seems to close in on herself and turns slowly to me. Her eyes, usually lively and expressive, now appear clouded with sorrow. Her brows are furrowed, and lines of distress are etched across her forehead. The corners of her mouth are downturned, and her lips quiver with emotion, as if trying to contain the depth of her feelings. My face instantly drops and I begin to fear that I made a joke in ill taste.

"Oh my Gods, Rita! What happened? Are you okay?!" I slowly move toward her but she takes a step back, shaking her head. Her face softens as she takes in my features.

"Lo siento....." her voice barely an audible whisper before she claps me on the back and walks out of the changing area.

I stare at her retreating back, my mouth agape. I have never seen Rita show any sort of despondency, and now she is uncommonly soft spoken and giving me a wide berth. I drop my gym bag into my locker and plop onto a nearby bench. The dull oak wooden seat creaks beneath me and reverberates throughout the locker room along with my dejected sigh. I'm used to the rest of the precinct being callous toward me, but Rita has never treated me this way. She's not being mean, necessarily, but she's never avoided me like this.. I rub my palms into my eyes trying to clear the bleariness from my vision. I stare blankly at the lockers in front of me for a few minutes before pushing off the bench and heading toward my desk.

As I make my way there, I force myself to be as quiet as possible. The sudden change in everyone's demeanor today makes me to want to melt into a puddle and disappear. The floor beneath my feet seems to creak ever so slightly, making me wince with each step. I tiptoe, taking careful strides, trying to minimize any noise that might draw attention to me. But isn't that what I wanted? I want my comrades to acknowledge my existence or at least go back to the way it was yesterday. I would even gladly take Jimmy's snarky-ass comments towards me if it meant someone spoke to me.

The sound of my footsteps echo noticeably throughout the unusually quiet space, making me wince inadvertently. Even the slightest rustling of my clothes as I adjust them has me feeling self-conscious, afraid that it might disrupt the unnatural stillness of the station. With each passing moment, my heart beats a little faster, as if in sync with my determination to maintain this hushed atmosphere. I hold my breath at times, trying to silence any involuntary sounds that might escape.

As I approach my desk, I reach out gently to retrieve my chair, lifting it ever so carefully to avoid the telltale scraping sound. Once seated, I settle myself, ensuring my belongings are arranged neatly and silently. I open my computer with the utmost care and grit my teeth at the startup chime. I don't know why I am being purposefully quiet. Our office is generally a hustle and bustle of sounds and alarms going off, but today? Today it is as if a sound deafening veil has blanketed our precinct and everyone, myself included, is afraid to make a peep.

The case load from the last few homicides still weighs heavily on my mind and I'm reminded of Dad's reaction to my mentioning the victims. I begin to type on the keyboard with a lighter touch than usual, cognizant of the soft clicking sounds that accompany each keystroke. The stillness encircles me, and I find myself focusing intently on my tasks, afraid that any sound I make will disrupt the somber tomb that has become the precinct. It becomes a balancing act between getting my work done efficiently and being as unobtrusive as possible. Both of which I am failing at miserably as my mind jumps from task to task.

I click through the various files of our victims, reading over each report carefully to see if they have any other connections besides their similar criminal histories.

And my dad being the lead on both cases, of course.

But Dad was a cop for many *many* years, so it could just be a coincidence that he ended up working on these. I can't seem to find anything beyond their arrests for sexual assault on a minor.

So, maybe it was the same bust. That's the most logical explanation.

But why wouldn't Dad answer any questions about it? What is it about these particular cases that makes him so irate when I bring them up? I sigh at the thought of all the valuable information I could garner from him, if only he would cooperate.

Okay. Let's start from the beginning—their original arrest—and try to piece this shit show together.

I click open Bradley Chancler's file first and slowly read over the notes, reports, crime scene photos, and sentencing from the judge.

Bradley Chancler, twenty-five, Caucasian male. Tried with solicitation of sexual acts to a minor under the age of ten, lewd and lascivious acts on a minor under the age of ten; pleaded guilty to a lesser charge for possession of crack-cocaine in the amount of fifty grams with intent to sell. Bradley was sentenced to ten years for drug trafficking and ten years for child molestation to be served consecutively.

I peer at his mugshot, making mental comparisons between the younger version in his photo and the man I ran into just hours before he was murdered. Even in his photo from two decades ago, the same general feeling of unease overwhelms me. The bastard doesn't even look ashamed of his crimes in the photo. In fact, he has a disgustingly smug look on his face. His deep-brown eyes flashing a look that would make the devil himself recoil. This human is pure evil and I can't help but thank the Gods that he is no longer alive and cannot hurt another child ever again. Twenty years was not nearly enough for the amount of trauma and damage he did to those children.

"Thanks to whomever took the trash out," I mutter to myself as I continue to read one disgusting report on Chancler after the other.

The keys on my keyboard clack loudly in the near-silence of the precinct as I begin my search for information on Davit Petrosyan, the second victim of our potential serial killer. Davit doesn't look any different in his mugshot from when he was arrested over twenty years ago than he did when I ran into him on the streets just the other day. He had the same tan and deep set, soulless eyes. My skin crawls again at the recollection of his words the day I ran into him on the street.

There is something about this man that makes every instinct in me scream as loud as possible. Suddenly, though, within a moment of that panic setting in, a wash of relief hits me. I don't even know what to do with these conflicting emotions anymore, but this huge jump from panicking to complete stillness is too much for me to wrap my head around. Perhaps it is the knowledge that he, like Chancler, is also dead and can't hurt anyone anymore? That has always been the worst part of the job, knowing there are creeps out there that hurt the innocent. Unfortunately, it is also what keeps me employed. I scan the rap sheet of the deceased man, noting all the similarities he and Bradley shared in crimes and sentencing.

Charged with child molestation and possession of crack-cocaine with intent to sell.

Even the length of their sentencing was the same.

I dig deeper into both men's files, but unfortunately I am met with wall upon wall of blocked information. The only factor that ties these two men together is that my dad was the arresting officer.

I won't sit here and lie that I feel any sort of remorse that these two heinous individuals are no longer among the living. I will just have to suck it up and try to fit the puzzle pieces together to make sure this serial killer doesn't strike innocent people. I sigh heavily, resting my elbows on my desk and pressing the heels of my palms into my eyes.

I glance around the room and see Rita steadily typing away on her keyboard and comparing notes in a file she has opened in front of her. I grab the files I have on my desk, making my way toward my partner to make an attempt at normalcy.

"Hey, Rita. Have you found anything to help figure out who's sending these men to meet their maker?"

Rita looks up from her screen, a flicker of emotion flitting across her face before returning back to her neutral expression. "Not really. I can't seem to get past the redactions. I will have to ask Dubris if he is able to recover them."

"Given the message found at each crime scene, it is possible that it is the previous victims of their assaults seeking their own justice, or maybe loved ones of these victims."

"That would make the most sense, but until we know exactly who the redacted minor is, we can't even begin to seek them out to ask questions."

A throat clears from behind me and I jump, spinning around quickly. Behind me, a slightly overweight balding man stands a few paces from where Rita and I are hunched over our case files, his arms clasped in front of himself wringing his hat in his hands. I straighten up, my focus shifting between him and Rita. His voice, which normally carries an air of authority, is now soft spoken and almost fearful. This subtle shift in his demeanor alone is enough to make the hairs on the back of my neck stand on end.

"Excuse me," he says, his tone firm but not unkind. "Can I speak to you in my office?"

Rita jumps up next to me and takes a step in the captain's direction, but he stops her by holding up his hand. I look at her, an unspoken understanding happening between us, and nod, fear setting in as I become distinctly aware of the entire precinct's eyes now on me. Beyond Rita's "I'm sorry" earlier this morning, Captain Dubris is the first person to acknowledge my existence today.

Am I getting fired?

My entire body starts to feel like it is being weighed down by a thousand-pound anchor. My limbs are weak and heavy with dread and it is taking everything in me to trudge along behind my mentor. I begin to go over every interaction I've had with the captain—and even my subordinates—trying to figure out where I went wrong, where I might have fucked up so royally that I now find myself in this situation with my boss. A million scenarios play out in my head, each one a more outlandish reason for being sacked than the next.

Captain Dubris pushes his office door open and ushers me into the room. The walls are lined with shelves stacked high with law enforcement manuals, commendations, and a collection of stern-looking portraits of past police captains, a photo of a younger version of my dad among them. He is the epitome of health in the picture, his black hair cut into a high and tight with his warm-sepia skin looking vibrant and full of life. A stark contrast to the man holed up in the hospital bed a few miles from here. A frown crosses my lips as the thought sits like a stone upon my heart. The captains' desk dominates the center of the room, its polished surface reflecting the soft light filtering through half-drawn blinds. His desk is almost completely bare, save for the computer monitor, a single photo of his family, and a stack of reports piled neatly in the center.

Dubris motions for me to sit on the plush leather and wood chair that's in front of his desk. The unusually anxious man slumps into his chair behind the desk and stares at me with sorrowful eyes. Years of being on the job suddenly seems to have chiseled itself into every line on his face. The tension in the air feels so thick that I can't seem to breathe without making a conscious effort. Another overwhelming wave of dread hits me, and I feel beads of sweat forming on my forehead despite the cool air conditioning.

"Captain, I-I'm sorry for whatever I did!" I begin to stammer and start rattling off whatever nonsense I can think of that might *potentially* be my fault.

Was it my OCD that finally did me in?

Was it the attitude I keep giving Jimmy? Even though he's an asshole and deserves every bit of it. I won't even begin to apologize for that.

Was it because of my moral compass that always seems to differ from my colleagues?

My brain begins to pick apart every case I've ever worked on, every interaction I've had with anybody at any point in time. I'm spinning stories faster in my head than I can even comprehend or begin to rationalize that those aren't probably it. Whatever is going on today in the office is suffocating me and I can't keep my composure for much longer before I begin to spiral.

The captain holds his hand up in a silent gesture telling me to close my mouth. then sighs deeply.

"No, no, Delilah. None of that." He seems to be at a loss for words, a state I have never once seen him in during the entire decade we've worked together. "There's no easy way to say this but—"

"But I'm fired...," I interject as my chest falls. I knew this was coming. I should've seen the signs. I knew my eating disorder and compulsions would catch up to me.

"What? No! Delilah..." He doesn't seem to be able to get the words out. It's as if all forms of speech just elude him and he is visibly struggling with what to say. But if I'm not fired, then what is it?

"Captain?" I lean closer to the edge of my seat, showing that I am listening and awaiting any instructions he needs to give.

"There's no easy way to say this but..." he sighs heavily, whatever he has to say clearly weighing on him. "I got a call from the hospital early this morning, and your father passed away in the middle of the night."

CHAPTER FOURTEEN

"I'm sorry, come again?" My ears must be deceiving me. This has to be some sort of sick prank, but why the department would do this to me is beyond my comprehension right now. It's like my entire brain has just ceased to process anything.

"Delilah..." Dubris speaks even more softly than before, his voice in a pitch I have only ever heard him use with victims' loved ones. Everything around me begins to blur and the pressure in my ears builds to where it sounds like I am underwater. I can see the captain's lips moving but I cannot understand a word that is coming out of his mouth. The whole world has come to a screeching halt. It has just stopped turning and I am stuck in a loop of disbelief. It's officially Groundhog Day and I am the star of the show.

The words echo in my ears, but they refuse to settle in my consciousness. I keep waiting for someone to tell me it is all a cruel joke or a misunderstanding, because the idea of my dad not being in this world anymore is just too unthinkable. He is—*was?*—my lifeline. My very best friend. The rock holding my entire world together since Mom passed away. My heart aches at the news, and every fiber of my being resists accepting the reality that was just been unceremoniously thrust upon me. My brain has activated a defensive mechanism that is trying to protect me from the overwhelming onslaught of emotions that is sure to follow if I allow myself to believe it. A tidal wave that will no doubt drown me should the dam break. It's funny how the mind can create this barrier between what you know to be true and what you're capable of comprehending.

In that moment, I am trapped between knowing and understanding, yet unable to bridge the gap between the two.

"Delilah...?" The balding gentleman before me speaks again, this time a little louder, urging my attention toward him. "Are you all right?"

Am I all right? AM I ALL RIGHT?! What an asinine question for someone, *anyone*, to ask in this situation, let alone the person who delivered the unfathomable news. In what realm would anyone be "all right"? I can't believe what I am hearing. My heart is pounding, my hands are clenched into fists, and a surge of anger courses through me like a wildfire. I have just been bombarded with the news of my dad's passing after being ostracized most of the morning. How could I be *all right*?! The weight of those words still hang heavy in the air, suffocating me with grief, and yet this simple question from my mentor seems infuriatingly insensitive.

"Are you all right?" Captain Dubris asks again, his tone laced with an irritating mix of concern and detachment. It is as if he couldn't be bothered to truly grasp the magnitude of what he has just dropped onto my lap. As if that token question—the question that seems to be on everyone's lips the moment anyone is met with horrible news—could even come close to addressing the tornado of emotions swirling within me.

"All right?" *I snap back, my voice sharper than I intend. "Does it look like I'm all right? You dropped the bomb on me that my dad died, and you're asking if I'm all right?!" My voice trembles with anger, and I can feel my cheeks burning.*

At least, that's what I want to lash out. That's what I want to scream and shout at the top of my lungs from every rooftop as I collapse to my knees like they do in those black-and-movies while a torrential downpour barrages me ferociously with rain.

But I don't.

I just stare blankly at my mentor trying to force words to form, trying to allow anything to escape my throat—a sob, a wail, a curse to the heavens, *anything.*

Dubris furrows his brows, his steel eyes scanning my face for any resemblance of emotions or reaction. I stare past him, his squat frame beginning to shape into a formless blob as I dissociate from this hell on earth. Maybe he is trying to be compassionate, trying to check up on the "problem child," the unhinged one of the precinct, but at this moment, his question feels like a slap in the face. How dare he reduce my pain, my grief, my loss, to a mere "are you all right?" How can he not see that I am anything but all right?

I take a deep, shuddering breath, struggling to regain some semblance of composure, to lose the dissociated, glossy-eyed gaze. "I, uh, I appreciate your concern," I say, my voice meek, with a touch of resignation. "I'll...I'll be all right," I lie through my teeth. It's all I can say in this moment as my brain is still trying to comprehend those few simple words that took my dad away from me forever.

There is an awkward silence, and I can sense his discomfort. He probably hadn't expected such a blasé reaction, but I don't care. In this moment, my disconnection is a shield, a defense mechanism against the overwhelming pain threatening to consume me. As the seconds that feel like hours tick by, Captain's expression softens, and his eyes no longer seem to be scanning my face for the grief he so clearly expected to take hold of me. Maybe, just maybe, he buys the lie. Maybe he is thinking of using this as an excuse to finally get me off the force. Now that my dad isn't around, he has no obligation to uphold the promise he made to him all those years ago.

Eventually, he nods, his voice more even in tone. "I'm really sorry for your loss, Delilah. Your dad was a great man. One that I looked up to and thanked the Lord every day that I got to train underneath. If there's anything I can do, anything you want to talk about, I'm here."

I absentmindedly nod back. I'm not sure what to do or where to go from here, but now I am beginning to wonder why the hospital called Captain Dubris instead of me. I hold Dad's power of attorney and am next of kin. When did Dad change the forms so I am not the first person notified? And what steps do I take now to plan for his funeral, or to handle his house and belongings? I prayed and hoped with all my might that he would leave that hospital bed and go back to my childhood home. The quaint sunflower-yellow house with its neatly manicured lawn. The one where

I lived out my formative years, where my fondest childhood memories were formed and I found my forever family. Now I have to make that trek alone and deal with all of the emotional turmoil that's going to come with it.

"Is that all, Captain?" I say flatly. I don't know how much longer I can keep it together if I stay in this office.

Captain Dubris sighs and the lines on his face seem to deepen. "Yes. Please take the rest of the day off and take as long as you need. Hernandez can handle the case load on her own."

My steps are calculated as I make my way to the solid oak door, its brass door knob showing the tarnish of years of use. The hollow expression on my face catches my attention in the warped reflection of the handle, and I don't even recognize myself. I steal a cursory glance over my shoulder at Captain Dubris sitting hunched over his desk, pen in hand, scratching away at whatever document is laid out in front of him.

"Why were you called?"

The scratching stops and out of the corner of my eye I see him look up.

"Why were you called?" I repeated, voice void of any emotion.

"Your dad called me a week ago and told me he changed the next of kin contact to me so you wouldn't be alone when the call came," Dubris's voice cracks at the last sentence.

I give a solitary nod before sliding out of the office to go grab whatever effects are still in my locker. Rita is waiting for me on the bench in the locker room and when she sees me she jumps up.

"Delilah..."

I snap my head in her direction, my eyes shooting daggers at her before slamming my locker shut. I race to the safety of my car and the three locks that protect me from the outside world. I grip the steering wheel, staring blankly through my windshield, driving on autopilot.

My tiny apartment has never felt so big and empty. The place I used to seek solace in and enjoy the calm and quiet of has now made me feel so alone and isolated. Dropping my bag onto the floor just inside the door, I lean against the cool wood and stare at the wall of pictures Dad helped me put up when I first moved into this space. The images seem to take on a life of their own as the people, the places, and the memories attached to them are suddenly projected in the space before me like an old movie. A flash of a younger version of my parents dancing at their wedding glides across my living room floor in between the images of the three of us laughing and smiling at the zoo shortly after I was adopted. Everyone was so happy, so carefree.

Alive.

The thought of both of my parents, my saviors, being taken from me suddenly hits me like a ton of bricks and the flood gates open. I lunge at the pictures on the wall, screaming in the most gut-wrenching, earth-shattering scream that has ever escaped my lips. Before I can stop myself, I start to yank the picture frames off the wall and fling them haphazardly around my apartment. Blinding hot tears stream down my face as all the pent up anguish is no longer contained in my slender frame. When there are no more photos left for me to rip off the walls, I look around the disarrayed state of my sanctuary and sink to my knees in the middle of all the broken glass and wooden frames.

My face is flushed and my chest is heaving as I continue to wail, begging and pleading with whatever God is listening to please bring my mom and dad back to me. I may be thirty-five, but I can't do this on my own.

By the time I have finished crying, it's not for a sudden lack of feeling the grief and loss, but rather because I physically have no more tears left in my body, no more voice to scream with. My eyes are swollen and my nose red and crusted with snot. Shattered glass and photographs litter the floor creating a crime scene of their own. The victim? All the tarnished memories, and the chance of future memories with the two people who mean more to me than anyone else in this world. There is no one to convict for these crimes, no one to put through a trial for ripping a family apart. There is no evidence to collect, no closure for those left behind.

For me. I am the family member left behind in the cruel wake of death. Not that Death was senseless with his choosing because, logically, I know Dad was hurting. I know he wanted nothing more than to be with Mom again, to be free of pain. And I wanted that for him! I wanted him to be free of pain and to be with the love of his life again. I just didn't want to be left alone. Again.

I feel so helpless. I feel the same way I did when I was placed in the foster system after I was taken away from my birth parents. Except, this time, there are no guardian angels in the guise of loving parents coming to save me. There is no one coming to rescue a scared, lonely thirteen-year-old little girl cleverly disguised as a thirty-five-year-old woman. There is no one coming to rescue *me*.

CHAPTER FIFTEEN

It has been nearly a week since Captain Dubris told me of my dad's passing and, even though my phone tells me five days have passed, internally it feels like a millennium. And at the same time, it feels as if time has stood still. Captain Dubris and Rita swung by the day after the news broke to bring me soup (which still sits on the counter, now cold and with a film on the surface of the liquid) and to help clean up the shattered remains of my picture frames. Jericho stopped by yesterday—or was it the day before?—to offer his condolences. Who it was that actually told him is still a mystery to me, but it helped to have a familiar face around as I began to navigate the details of Dad's funeral arrangements and his estate. Beyond these three humans, I have not seen another living soul since I ran out of the precinct. I'm not sure if I should be grateful or unnerved that no one else has checked on me.

The bags under my eyes have darkened to a royal purple and the puffiness from crying still hasn't abated. I have slept more in the last few days than I have in the last month and, while I should feel thankful that I'm catching up on my sleep, the night terrors are becoming unavoidable, more visceral, and more agonizing. I wish I could say the screaming little girl has disappeared from my subconscious, but her presences has only become more pronounced. Even in my waking hours I can hear her screaming and crying for help. A little girl that I finally got proof of doesn't even exist outside of these four walls. She's always crying for her mother and father to help her or to "please stop." And in the dreams where I'm not being terrorized by this unseen child, my mind is torturing me with Dad's last moments in the hospital where I interrogated him to the point of a seizure from the stress. The medical abnormality that he never recovered from.

The most recent nightmare involving Dad has me running down a dimly lit hospital hallway. I can see him on his bed, the lights surrounding him garishly bright. He looks so frail and paler than I've ever seen him. Any time I try to approach him, to hold his hand or kiss his forehead, I am instead met with racing down a never ending hallway. His bed getting farther and farther away. It's like running on a treadmill—constantly in motion, but the runner never actually makes it to their destination.

I always bolt upright, drenched in sweat, bawling my eyes out and panting when I have these ones. But alas, I am met with not even a moment's peace. As soon as I get my bearings from this nightmare, the little girl screaming for help starts to echo through my apartment again. Ear plugs and burying my head under my pillows and blankets don't deafen the sound at all. I cry myself back to sleep and pray to the Gods for at least one night where I am not haunted by this little girl and her misery. I fear that if this continues much longer, I will be next in the grave.

But no one will mourn me.

S orrow and disbelief press upon me from all sides as I stand among a sea of mourners at my father's funeral. The air is thick with grief, and the sky overhead matches the somber mood, draped in clouds that threaten rain. It's as if even nature herself weeps for the loss we've suffered.

I try to keep my composure, but my trembling hands betray the emotions coursing through me. The tears are just beneath the surface, ready to spill at any moment. The sight of the casket, a polished mahogany box draped with a pristine American flag, is a stark reminder that my dad is really gone. My uncle, the only remaining relative of Dad's (whom I haven't seen in months), holds my hand as his own lip quivers at the loss of his younger brother.

The service begins, and the words of the officiant are a distant murmur in my ears. Memories of my father flash before my eyes like a flickering film reel. His laughter, his advice, his unwavering support—they all swirl together, making it hard to comprehend that he won't be there anymore.

I look around at the people gathered here. Friends, family, and acquaintances have all come to pay their respects. Their faces are a mixture of sympathy and sorrow, and I appreciate their presence, even though it feels strange to see them in this context. It is amazing to see the entire precinct here to honor Dad's memory. Captain and Rita organized the service beautifully, right down to gun salute as we lay him in the ground in the same plot Mom is buried in.

As the officiant speaks about my father's life, I'm struck by the depth of his impact on so many lives. The stories shared by friends and his old coworkers paint a vivid picture of a man who was not just my father, but a mentor, a friend, and a pillar of strength to others as well. I feel a strange sense of pride knowing that he was loved and admired by so many. The eulogies offer moments of solace amidst the overwhelming grief. Listening to others share their memories of my dad, their anecdotes and heartfelt words, I realize that his legacy will continue on in the hearts and minds of all those that he touched. His kindness, his wisdom, and his love have left an indelible mark on all of us.

The officiant motions for my fellow officers to proceed to the designated area to begin the twenty-one gun salute. The air around us stills. I jump with each fire of the rifles, tears falling with every blast. The shots come to an end, their echo continuing faintly off in the distance. A minimal trace of smoke and sulfur permeates the air. The clicks of the officers' dress shoes on the sidewalk rebounds through the surrounding areas in soft taps. Captain Dubris and Rita have donned their honor guard uniforms, the navy blue garments creased just so. An older gentleman in the same, crisp uniform somberly places the shiny, gold bugle to his lips and a low, melodic tune penetrates the air.

The protocol for this honorary service is seamless. It's a well-oiled machine built upon the lives of those that have left us behind. I can feel my uncle's body tremble as he tries to hold himself together. Whether it's for me or for himself, I'm not sure. I am so lost in my own grief that everything around me blurs from the tears. Someone makes a low, throat clearing noise in front of me snapping me back to the present, the one place I don't want to be right now. I blink through the pain, my sorrow spilling down my cheeks, and I'm met with a pair of mournful gray eyes.

"On behalf of a grateful nation, we thank you for your loved one's service," Captain Dubris says stoically, but his eyes are full of compassion. In between a pair of pristine, white cotton gloves is the flag that was only moments ago draped over the beautiful mahogany casket that is now my dad's final resting place. I gingerly take the flag from Captain's hands and press it to my chest, hugging it tightly and burying my head into the cloth in a feeble attempt to be as close as possible to my late best friend.

There's no stopping the tears now. Uncontrollable wails escape my chapped lips as I curl into the flag, my whole body shuddering. My uncle drapes himself over my crumpling body, holding onto me as we both succumb to our grief.

As the service nears its end, the casket is slowly lowered into the ground ceremoniously.

I place a single rose on top, a symbol of my love and gratitude. It's a painful moment, watching the earth swallow my whole heart for a second time. It takes all of my strength to not collapse onto the casket and wail like a child begging and pleading for all the Gods in the universe to please take me with him, to take me to the Otherside to be with my parents again. I try to keep my decorum even as my eyeliner and mascara streak and smudge my face.

The sound of dirt being shoveled into the grave is a harsh reality. The subtle *thump* of each shovel-full against the wood seems louder than it should be. Everything is somehow both louder and impossibly distant and my mind is unable to make sense of it all. But that's just it, grief and death aren't supposed to make sense. I take a handful of the soft, damp earth and let it slip through my fingers, a symbolic farewell to my beloved father. I stay stationary, watching the slowly filling grave, the surreal symbolism of dirt and worms and time engulfing my two best friends not lost on me. Claps on my back follow after each mourner says their final farewell, tears staining their cheeks as well.

As we cross through the cemetery gates to head back to reality, I take one last look behind me at the freshly covered mound. I'm acutely aware of the void that now exists in my heart. The pain of this loss is profound, and I'm not sure how I will recover from this when almost twenty years later, I am still trying to heal from losing my mom. I glance at my uncle, his face crestfallen and eyes swollen from crying. I'm trying to find the right words to say, to tell him how sorry I am for his loss. For *our* loss, as if my pain wasn't just as evident. To tell Uncle Carson anything that would help either of us in this process.

But nothing comes.

Nothing will ever come, because there are no words to ease the pain of a heart broken by grief.

I lean my head against the cool window and hug my dad's flag tightly to my chest, closing my eyes against the setting sun and willing myself back to a time where I had both of my parents and my life wasn't a walking nightmare.

CHAPTER SIXTEEN

I stand before the familiar old house, its weathered, pale-yellow façade bearing witness to the passage of time. Even though Dad has been in the hospital for the last few months, the lawn is still neatly manicured with the help of some neighborhood kid I pay weekly. Despite the neighbors lawns turning various shades of beige and brown under the San Diego summer sun, his lawn is always lush and green. I guess that's just something you keep up with when you retire. This lawn was Dad's pride and joy, and I couldn't let that start to wither and die too. I kept trying to keep up appearances, a subconscious promise to myself that Dad was going to get better and come back to this house as if he never left. Now the evening sun casts long shadows across the front yard, stretching out toward me. The air is filled with a strange mix of nostalgia and sorrow, and my heart feels like lead as I take the first step up the front porch.

Days have passed since Dad's funeral and this is Uncle Carson's last night in town. He's insistent that he help me go through the house before he heads back to Pennsylvania. Apparently helping with this is (what feels like to me) monumental task is going to help his own grief. Or something like that. I don't really have the heart to tell him no and, realistically, I could use some company and advice on how to go forward with Dad's estate.

The key feels cold and foreign in my hand as I slide it into the lock, turning it with a creak that seems to echo through the house. The door swings open, revealing the gloomy, partially sun-lit interior. Dust motes dance in the slivers of sunlight that filter through the curtains, creating a melancholic ballet that mirrors the emotions swirling within me.

As I step into the foyer, memories flood back like a tidal wave. The scent of my childhood home, a blend of my mother's favorite flowers—hyacinths that Dad made sure to always have a bouquet of—and my father's old books surrounds me. The familiar groan of the wooden floorboards underfoot, each one bearing the marks of years gone by, welcome me back.

I make my way through the house, room by room, each space holding its own cherished memory. The kitchen where my mother taught me to bake her famous chocolate chip cookies now lays silent and cold. The living room, where my father regaled me with stories from his time in the force, now feels empty without his booming laughter. A thin layer of dust covers the picture frames that line the walls.

Upstairs, I hesitate outside the door to my childhood bedroom. Slowly, I push it open, and a rush of emotions washes over me. The room is frozen in time, with posters of my favorite bands still adorning the walls and a well-worn teddy bear sitting on the bed. It is as if my parents have just stepped out for a moment and will return at any second. I may have joined my parents later in my life, but they never made me feel any less. In fact, quite the contrary. They always reminded me that I was their pride and joy. They loved me like no other parents could.

I sink onto the edge of the bed, tears welling up in my eyes. Their absence burdens my heart and soul, nearly crushing me, but I find comfort in the memories that come flooding back. The countless bedtime stories, the late-night talks, and the whispered lullabies permeate the room, filling the empty spaces with their echoes. I bury my head in my hands for the umpteenth time today and sob uncontrollably. I had hoped and prayed that Dad would win his battle with cancer. It never occurred to me that once he was admitted to the hospital he would never make it out, that he would never come home again. I didn't know it would be the start of his death sentence.

Outside the window, the sun has dipped below the horizon, casting the room into darkness. It is time to face the reality of the present. My parents are gone, and this house is no longer a home. No longer *my* home. It is just a place filled with memories and ghosts of the past, a place where the past would forever be preserved if I left it as-is. I know I will never be able to set foot in here again without feeling the pain of the loss of my two best friends and so, I must get it ready for a new family to create memories in.

I push myself up off the bed and use my phone's flashlight to find the light switch. An eerie sensation washes over me and I get the feeling that I'm being watched. I cast a subtle glance over my shoulder and can see a shadowy figure standing outside my bedroom window, looking up from the street below. I jump out of my skin and quickly turn on the light, whirling around to face whoever is glaring up at the house. I rub my eyes, trying to force them into focus after noticing there is no one on the street below now. I clearly must be exhausted and emotionally drained to be seeing things the way I have been. I shake my head, clearing the unease that settles across my skin, and make my way to Mom and Dad's room, flicking on the hallway light as I go.

Entering my parents' room is an emotional journey that I would've gladly avoided for the remainder of my life, but I know that I can't keep putting off the estate. Especially when Uncle Carson is here to help me manage everything before he goes back home.

The door creaks softly as I push it open, revealing a space that once held so much life and warmth. But now, walking through this room feels akin to walking through a museum, or perhaps an archeological site. Everything is just as it was, a silent testament to the loss that is still so raw. It somehow feels both as if they might walk in at any second and like not a soul has set foot in here in years. The room is bathed in the remaining soft, muted light of day, creating an aura of melancholy. Their bed, neatly made, appears untouched since the last time they slept here. This is surreal and I'm dying inside, wishing for them to walk back through the door.

I approach the dresser, where a collection of family photos stands in a row of frames, covered in the same thin layer of dust that coats nearly every surface in this once happy home. Each photo tells a different story, the past versions of ourselves captured on film like those insects trapped in amber. My parents in their wedding photo, their smiles radiating joy and promise. Our family on vacations, at holidays and birthdays, all now bittersweet reminders of the love and happiness we shared. Dad's signature scent of sandalwood and cedar still lingers in the room even though he hasn't been here in over three months. I open the closet, and the sight of their clothes neatly hung or folded takes my breath away. Dad never could get rid of Mom's clothes after all these years and, if it wasn't for Uncle Carson, I never would've been able to come back here and everything would remain as it is until the day I die. I run the fabric of one of Mom's sundresses through my fingers, and images of her kneeling in the garden tending to her flowers with the dress flowing around her dance across my mind's eye.

I sit down on their bed, my fingers grazing the soft bedspread. More flashbacks consume me—late-night talks, moments of comfort during tough times, and the times they'd sit in this very spot to just hold me when I needed a good cry and escape from the bullies at school. Tears threaten to fall once more as I relive the worst days of my life over and over again. I need to keep moving or I'm going to end up catatonic again which will get me nowhere. And the time that I'll actually have help with all this is becoming increasingly limited.

Turning to their nightstands, I find the familiar items they cherished. My mother's worn-out journal, countless pages filled with her thoughts and dreams. My father's reading glasses resting on a book, one he never got to finish.

I pick up a frame containing a picture of my dad and me on my graduation day from the academy. Held firmly against my chest is another framed photo, one of Mom. After she died, Dad and I always used this photo as her stand-in even though it never took the place of the real thing. That photo of her will always be my favorite. It wasn't from her wedding day, or even from the day I was adopted. My favorite photo, the one I would always beg Dad to bring on every vacation so we could still have memories of her, was the one Dad candidly shot of her working in the flower beds out front. Her bright red hair gleaming in the sunlight, a light flush to her pale cheeks. Her smile is so radiant, crinkles forming at the corner of her eyes from laughing so hard.

The tears fall again as I clutch the photo to my chest, sobs echoing down the hallway.

"Hey, kiddo." Uncle Carson is in the doorway, his words soft and his eyes red and puffy.

I look up at him, sniffling, "Hey..."

"Why don't you go take a break. I'll go through the stuff in here and figure out what we're keeping and what should be sold or donated."

I nod, giving him a tight squeeze. Leaving their room is a heavy step, like saying goodbye all over again. It's a stark reminder of the emptiness they've left behind. I slowly make my way back down to the living room, plopping on the sofa. As the old wooden frame creaks softly under my weight, I look around the living room, taking it all in. Every last nook and cranny; every chip in the wall paper; every dust particle floating in the air.

Everything.

I slowly stir, my eyes heavy with sleep, as I become aware of my surroundings. The room is shrouded in darkness, and the only light seeping through is from upstairs. I must have fallen asleep on the couch. It was the first time in a long while that I've fallen asleep without the onslaught of nightmares. I still don't feel any more rested, but the reprieve from listening to the phantom little girl was nice. I rub my eyes to clear away the last traces of sleep. The soft hum of the refrigerator in the corner of the attached kitchen provides a gentle background noise, while the ticking of a nearby clock seems louder than usual in the quiet of the night.

I glance toward the staircase, where the dim glow of the hallway light spills down, casting eerie shadows on the living room floor. It's enough to reveal the familiar contours of the room, the bookshelves lined with well-worn novels, the coffee table with a scattering of magazines, and the cozy throw blanket that I assume Uncle Carson covered me with at some point after I fell asleep.

Reluctantly, I rise from the couch, the coolness of the hardwood floor beneath my feet a stark contrast to the warmth of the blanket. I make my way to the bottom of the stairs and stare up at the dim light coming from the floor above. Out of the corner of my eye, a shadow walks along one of the walls, causing me to jump.

It's probably just Uncle Carson, you dolt, I reprimand myself rather harshly.

Probably? *Probably?!* Who else could possibly be in my father's home?! When did all of the deductive reasoning skills I learned in police training drain out of my body? The only logical explanation for my extreme skittishness is grief and delirium caused by sheer exhaustion. Yeah. That has to be it.

I climb back up the stairs for a second time today, keeping a keen ear out for any unusual sounds. Upon the landing, I glance around at the open doors, hoping to see Uncle Carson or even his shadow to indicate that it was him who I saw rushing across the hallway just moments ago.

"Uncle Carson?" I call out, my voice echoing up the stairwell. "Are you up here?"

Without warning, a crashing sound comes from overhead. My hand subconsciously jolts to my hip, reaching for my gun. Then it clicks in my head. I just came from my dad's funeral. Why the fuck would I have my gun on me? I roll my eyes at my stupidity. At least *that* part of training decided to kick in.

I take a deep breath in and slowly exhale as I approach the drop down stairs that lead to our tiny attic. I begin cautiously climbing the rickety wooden steps, being careful not to arouse anyone uninvited that might be lurking in the space above. The scent of old wood and dust fills my nose, a familiar and comforting aroma that hasn't changed since I was a kid. My head crests the threshold as I turn on my phone's flashlight, and I'm suddenly sent rocketing into the past.

The light bounces off the small, cobweb-covered window illuminating the dust that lingers in the air. Boxes, stacked haphazardly, line the walls, each one a treasure trove of memories waiting to be unearthed. I move cautiously, my footsteps reverberating throughout the otherwise silent space. I feel around for the light switch and upon finding one, I try flicking it on to no avail.

I try again a few more times for good measure.

Nope. Still not working.

I'm not sure what part of the human brain has everyone wired to try the light switch multiple times when nothing happens. It bears the same result with each flick. Regrettably, this trait didn't miss me either.

The air is laden with the memory of years gone by. Old furniture draped in dusty sheets sits untouched. It's seriously a wonder how these pieces even got up here! A box labeled "Childhood Toys" catches my eye, and I eagerly open it, abandoning my original mission—against my better judgement—to investigate the mysterious noise I heard up here. Inside, I find an assortment of forgotten treasures: action figures, board games, and a well-loved teddy bear with one eye missing. Holding that teddy bear in my hands, I'm transported back to countless nights when it was my loyal companion, guarding me from imaginary monsters under the bed.

I close the box back up and slowly spin around with my phone's flashlight, unsure of what I am looking for, when some old, tattered boxes with a case number and my dead name catch my eye. I step over and around the various bits and bobs, careful to where I place my foot for fear that the flooring underneath might not be stable. I kneel before the box, trying to remove the tape with my one free hand and failing miserably. I search around for somewhere to prop my phone up when the floorboards behind me creak and the space around me darkens in shadow.

I jump up, spinning around, and in my clumsiness, I trip over the boxes I was just looking at. I grapple for my phone that dropped out of my hand and point it toward the shadowy figure that looms in front of me.

"Jericho?!"

CHAPTER SEVENTEEN

Standing before me is the man I have known my entire childhood, shadows landing harshly on his face. Something about the way they fall across his gaunt, haggard features sends chills down my spine. I have never seen this man look so menacing in the whole two decades I've known him. My mind is reeling as I wonder how he got into my parents' house without anyone knowing and how he even knew Uncle Carson and I were here.

"What are you doing here?! How did you—" I'm nearly speechless. I keep repeating myself, stammering over my words.

"You shouldn't be here, Del." As he speaks, his features begin to contort with his every shift into and out of the light from my phone, and my heart starts to race. The once familiar face I knew so well now appears distorted, almost grotesque, as the shadows seem to warp his expressions.

"What do you mean? This is my *dad*'s house! Why *shouldn't* I be here?!" I snap at him with a little more force than I mean to, but his statement is just completely absurd! If anything, *he* shouldn't be here. Or, at least, he should be able to tell me *why* he's here.

"It's dangerous for you to be here, Del. You need to run."

I try to focus on his words, to push away the irrational fear that is building inside me, but the dancing shadows that surround him hold me captive. It is as if a malevolent force is at play, turning a dear friend into something unrecognizable. Every twitch of his lips and every movement of his eyes cast eerie patterns on his face, creating an unsettling illusion. The lack of proper sleep and diet are surely to blame for my irrational behavior, as well as whatever trickery my phone's light is playing on me.

"Run? Why the fuck would I run? What are you blabbering on about?!"

Jericho takes a step forward, the shadows growing longer across his face, and I attempt to scramble backward while not taking my eyes off him. I feel another chill creep down my spine, and I have to remind myself that it is just a trick of the light, that there is nothing to fear. This is Jericho. The man who waited with my mother all those years ago so she wouldn't die alone in the streets after the hit and run. The man who would defend me from the bullies and walk home with me when he was home on leave. The veteran who, despite my numerous attempts to repay him for helping my family, always looked out for me without recompense. And yet, with each passing moment, the shadows seem to grow darker, his face more twisted, and I can't shake the feeling that something sinister is lurking just beneath the surface, waiting to reveal itself. Something none of us saw all those years ago.

"You're not *safe* here, Delilah!" He gets inches from my face, spit hitting me on the cheeks as he emphasizes the word "safe".

I struggle to maintain my composure, to hide the rising panic within me, but the shadows have all but consumed my friend's face, and the fear that has taken hold of me is impossible to ignore. Just a few short days ago, he was clean shaven and showered, but tonight he looks like he found himself back at the bottom of a bottle.

"Why am I not safe, Jericho? What is going on? You're scaring me!" It's too late. The admission of my fear is out there in the open and I can't take it back. I've never been fearful of this man my entire life and now he's a complete stranger to me. Did my dad's death completely unhinge him?

He quickly spins around on his heels, throwing his hands up in the air, kicking boxes out of his way as he stomps around the attic. A nearly imperceptible crazed look on his face as I follow him with my flashlight.

"Why aren't you listening to me, *Delilah*?!" He spits my name out like it's venom on his tongue.

"I'm *trying* to listen, Jericho! I just don't understand! *Why* am I not safe?" My voice almost sounds pleading. And maybe I am. I'm not sure what I am doing anymore. The days preceding my dad's death have all but broken me and maybe I too am going a bit mad.

He lets out an aggravated grunt, yanking on his hair. He seems to be becoming more and more unglued by the moment, kicking the boxes out of his way as he paces around quicker and quicker. Some boxes split slightly at the seams from his rough mishandling while others slide violently across the floor, causing a loud ruckus.

"They're going to come for you! You need to *leave*! They're going to find you and there's no stopping them!"

"WHO IS AFTER ME!?" I stand quickly, shining my light directly at him. "Just fucking talk to me, Jericho! Quit with the head games and give me a fucking straight answer! *Who* is coming for me?!"

There are a lot of "whos" in my life given my line of work and not having any other information isn't going to help me. I wouldn't even know what to be on the lookout for to keep myself safe.

He takes three long strides until he's right in my face again. He smells of whiskey and like he hasn't bathed in days despite having a job and stable housing now. He holds up a shaking finger and just as he opens his mouth to speak, I hear Uncle Carson from down below calling for me. Jericho knocks the phone from my hands and it goes skittering into some boxes behind me, pushing me backward as he runs off. I try to catch myself, but end up twisting around clumsily and fall face first into a dusty armchair, sending a plume of dirt and debris flying into the air which causes me to go into a coughing fit. I wheel back around to face our long-time family friend only to be greeted with nothingness.

Where the fuck did he go?

The lights flicker on and I jerk my arm up to shield my eyes.

"Are you okay, Del? I heard crashing."

It's Uncle Carson and he somehow managed to get the attic light to work. He casts a sideways glance in my direction. I must be a sight to see—hair disheveled, entirely covered in all manner of filth from my fall into the chair.

"Ye-yeah. Just couldn't get the light to work and I tripped while trying to use my phone as a guide."

"I see..." He looks at me quizzically, inspecting me from head to toe. "Well, I got a few more mementos loaded into the car that I would like to take back home with me if that's okay?"

Of course it was okay. Uncle Carson is Dad's only living relative that I have. He could take whatever he wanted. It would be selfish of me to say no. Besides, beyond a few pictures and Mom and Dad's wedding bands, I don't think I would be able to stomach having any other memories of my parents in my home. The constant reminder of their death would surely be my downfall.

It's been a week since Uncle Carson went back to Pennsylvania and I'm still on paid-leave from the precinct. I have tried to convince Captain Dubris to put me back on the schedule, but he feels that I would be too reckless and might jeopardize my investigations. Especially with the most recent case that I was working on prior to dad's death. I've been keeping an eye on the papers to see if there have been any more murders while I'm on administrative leave but, surprisingly, San Diego has been unusually quiet in terms of crime. I should be grateful that the rampant crime sprees in my beloved city have calmed down, but I am afraid that this strange string of murders will end up a cold case. I know Rita is competent in her abilities as a detective, but this is *my* case. *Was* my case.

My nights are still just as sleepless, if not more so as I try to avoid hearing the little girl screaming and crying every time I close my eyes. It's getting louder and louder and Anne assures me every time I bring it up to her that there is no family living in the units on either side of me. She says grief will do strange things to a person, but I don't think she realizes that these haunting sounds started way before Dad died. They're just getting worse by the day. How people get through the days after they bury a loved one seems so incomprehensible. My waking moments are filled with onslaughts of tears and my nights are filled with tossing and turning and nightmares where I relive losing my parents all over again. The scenarios in which I lose them are all different, but the result is always the same—I can never save them. Sometimes I'm the thirty-something year old adult I am now and sometimes I am the scared little girl they adopted.

The sun is slowly creeping through my curtains, bright rays breaking up the darkness. I sit curled into the corner of my couch, where I haven't moved for the better part of a week. My hair is a tangled rat's nest and my body odor has permeated the room more than I care to admit. I really should get up and at least shower. Maybe that will help ease the tension that settles into my shoulders. But removing myself from the security of my down comforter and stripping out of my clothes means being able to see all of me. To see the scars, my bones protruding at odd angles as I've lost even more weight. I should be ecstatic at the prospect of the latter, but I know it'll never be enough. I'll never be where I need to be. I will never be fully in control of this side of me, and so I succumb to it and listen to the demons as they scream loudly in my head to jog until I puke.

I manage to peel myself off of the couch, dropping the blanket into a pile as I stand up, an indent of my small frame left behind from where I situated myself days ago. Like every time before, I check the lock on the front door and my living room window before making my way into my bathroom, flicking the lights on as I go. I crank the shower on as hot as I can stand it, steam rising up from behind the shower curtain. As I pull my tank top over my head, I catch a glimpse of my ribs in the mirror and instinctively my hand trails over the scars marring my porcelain skin.

My hand runs over the shiny markings and I suddenly feel like I'm being punched in the gut. My mind draws a blank when I try to conjure up the memory of how or what could've caused these markings, and that causes me more distress than the marks themselves. It is like a hazy fog shrouds my memories, obscuring the events leading up to this moment. I sit here, alone in a room filled with the disconcerting silence of the unknown, only the sound of the pouring water hitting the tile echoing back at me. My mind races, desperately trying to piece together fragments of a puzzle that is missing crucial pieces. How did I end up like this? What happened? The frustration wells up within me, and I can't shake the feeling of being lost in my own life. With both of my parents gone now, I will never get the answers I need about the life I lived before.

My parents were always well meaning when it came to telling me about my life in the "before times," as we used to joke. Mom and Dad would reassure me that once I turned eighteen, they would tell me about my past. Their reasoning was that I would be of legal age and would have a better understanding of the world and, if I so chose, I would be able to reach out to my birth parents. But after Mom died, Dad refused to talk about it. Any time I asked about it, he acted like he didn't hear me. Eventually I learned to stop asking.

The water runs ice cold before I step out and stare at the blurry reflection in the foggy mirror. A misty canvas, it reflects a distorted version of my own image. I reach out tentatively, my fingers making contact with the cool surface. As I trace a path, a streak emerges in the fog, revealing a glimpse of the reflection beneath. But it isn't my face that is looking back at me. A younger, smaller face with sunken-in cheeks beneath high cheekbones stares back at me. Her eyes pitch black and her face unnatural shades of blues, purples, and greens. Blood trickles out of her nose and goose eggs poke out from underneath her scraggly hair.

Tears slowly stream down this ghastly specter's face, her chapped and bloodied bottom lip trembling. I stare on, mouth agape unsure of what I am seeing. This scene in my mirror evokes something deep inside me and I have the irresistible urge to reach out and touch it, to prove to myself that what I'm seeing is not real. The reflection in the mirror mimics my moves and raises her hand in perfect synchronization with mine. Before my hand can touch the smooth, reflective surface, the little girl in the mirror begins to scream at the top of her lungs, causing me to fall backwards, slipping on the wet tile and slamming into the tub.

CHAPTER EIGHTEEN

My eyes flutter open, and the first thing I notice is the harsh, unyielding light above. It takes a moment for the world to swim back into focus, and as awareness slowly seeps in, a dull ache resonates through my head and back. Confusion creeps into the recesses of my mind as I try to make sense of my surroundings. A shiver runs down my spine as the realization hits that I am naked on my bathroom floor. My hand reflexively reaches to the back of my head, discovering a tender bump that throbs in rhythm with my heartbeat. I wince, carefully probing the area to assess the damage.

No blood. Well that's a positive.

The memory of the slip begins to surface. The vivid image of the bathroom wall and ceiling rushing away from me flashes in my mind, and I grimace at the recollection of the impact. My back protests as I tentatively shift my position, a sharp twinge shooting through me. A muttered curse escapes my lips as I realize the full extent of my misfortune. I must have hit my head and back pretty hard.

How long have I been lying here?

With a cautious effort, I cling to the bathroom counter, pulling myself into a standing position. The room tilts slightly as I steady myself. I glance hesitantly at the mirror, half-expecting to see the battered child staring back at me, but it is only my reflection that stares back. I look a little disheveled but no worse for wear. I take stock of the situation and a mixture of relief and frustration wash over me. No serious injuries it seems, but the throbbing ache and the stiffness in my back will serve as a constant reminder of my bathroom misadventure. It's probably nothing some ibuprofen and rest can't help to alleviate, even though I know police protocol dictates I go to the hospital, especially considering I fell unconscious. But I just don't want to go through the trouble, and I don't want anyone from work to know. I'm sure I'll be fine. With a defeated sigh, I drop my head and focus my gaze on the off-white counter top.

I really am cracking up.

Once I finally right myself, I make my way to the bedroom and dress in a pair of leggings and an oversized tee. My blond hair is in that weird in-between state of being both wet and dry but either way, it's a tangled mess. It's not dry enough to tie up, but still too wet to be able to brush without it feeling like I'm yanking my hair out from the knots. I pull down on my cheeks, stretching my bottom eyelids and blowing air out of my mouth with a dramatic *pffft*. I am so tired it feels like no amount of sleep will ever allow me to recoup what I have lost. And no amount of concealer will hide the deep purplish-blue of the dark circles that now make their home under my eyes..

Sleep has always been an elusive beast for me, but this is utterly ridiculous. Maybe it's not necessarily the messed up sleep schedule, but the fact that any time I try to sleep it's riddled with incomprehensible nightmares. Nightmares on repeat of both of my parents dying and the ever-present nightmare of hearing—and now suddenly seeing!—a little girl screaming for someone to help her. No. Not just *someone*. Her *parents*. Always begging her dad to stop. Always begging for her mom to stop him and help her.

Who is she?

To top it off, my waking hours aren't much better. The homicides I was working having a strange connection to my Dad, him refusing to tell me anything about it, and now his death, which has not only ensured that he can never tell me, but has also thoroughly destroyed me—it's all really draining, to put it mildly. I wonder if it would help ease my mind if I went back and grabbed the old case file boxes from Dad's attic. Uncle Carson told me to leave them alone, to use my paid convalescent leave to actually grieve and not worry about work. He tried to remind me that Rita, Captain Dubris, and the rest of the squadron know what they are doing. But I can't get my mind off of them. Boxes that should've been stored in the vault at work have somehow ended up stowed away in Dad's attic all this time. And they might contain the missing connection to the murders that have rocked this town in the last week or so.

Murders that stopped...when Dad died.

The air outside is sticky, a clear reminder that San Diego is not transitioning well from summer to fall. It has reached the part of the season where you need a jacket to keep the chill off of your skin in the morning, but then you start sweating before noon. Personally, I prefer when San Diego gets its shit together and has a cohesive weather day. A day where I can don an oversized sweater and be at that perfect temperature all day long. None of this back and forth nonsense that Southern California is known for.

Pulling back up to Dad's house, this time alone, feels even more surreal than the day I crossed the threshold with Uncle Carson. I hadn't dared to tell him about my run-in with Jericho up in the attic. He would probably assume I had gone mad, because how could anyone get in the house without either of us noticing? The biggest question that still plagues my mind is, how did Jericho make it back down the attic stairs without Uncle Carson noticing? How did he even know we were here?

I push open the door to a home that is no longer filled with warmth and love. Instead I'm met with stagnant warm air that puts a chill into my bones as I search for the memories that should occupy every space of my existence. But between the grief and the insomnia, I can't seem to find them. Just the smell of dust and stale air.

But that's okay. Today is not a day that I need to be succumbing to an overwhelming wash of emotions. I'm here for one thing and one thing only: to get those file boxes out of the attic.

The boxes that hold the key to the connection between Dad and these homicides.

The key to, hopefully, figuring out what was redacted in the digital files.

I traipse up to the attic, the stairs creaking beneath my feet. Centuries feel like they have passed since I was last up here when in reality it has only been a week. The attic feels much smaller than it did the night that Jericho materialized up here. The boxes I tripped over are still where they landed, a thin layer of dust starting to cover them again as they prepare to lay in their final resting place. I take stock of all the junk in the dusty crawl space that I still need to go through as I scan the area for what I came up here for.

There.

Sitting in the middle of the attic, light from the vents filtering down upon it like some sort of halo, illuminating all the dust particles as they dance in its presence like it is a God. Surprisingly, they don't appear to have any dust on them whatsoever. Almost as if they were placed up here as an afterthought. Like they were stored somewhere else to preserve their freshness while everything else in this space seems to have been forgotten. I bend down and scoop up the missing piece of this mystery that will make everything all make sense.

At least, that's what I keep telling myself.

Fumbling with the two oversized boxes in my hands, I carefully start making my way down the stairs when my breath hitches in my chest. There's someone downstairs. *Two* someones. My ears strain to pick up their conversation, but everything begins to sound muffled and far away, as if I was listening to their conversation through a conch shell. Tinny ringing in my ears and their voices a distant echo. A faint smell hangs in the air. I know this smell. But from where? I can't place it but its presence puts my whole body on edge.

I set the boxes back on the landing of the attic, careful not to make any noise that might alert the intruders to my presence. I pat around my waist instinctually looking for my weapon. *Shit.* Of course I wouldn't have it on me! Why would I? It's not like I expected myself to need it on what was supposed to just be a quick trip to pick up important mementos from my deceased father's house. I do a quick survey of the attic, praying to find anything I can use as a weapon against the intruders.

Nothing.

I'm not even sure what I was expecting to find anyway. What did I plan to do? Throw boxes at them down the stairs like Donkey Kong? I am becoming more and more delusional by the day. Years of training forgotten in a sea of grief. Maybe I really do need to take Uncle Carson's advice and relax. Maybe I should go visit him in Pennsylvania; get out of the city that, as of late, has been giving my psyche nothing but problems. It might be good for the soul. Or it might make everything worse being so far away from the last place I ever saw my parents.

As silently as I can, I creep down the rickety stairs, stopping a few steps from the bottom, begging the Gods to not let them do their notorious creak under my feet. Do I try to confront the invaders? Do I just plan to make an escape out the front door and drive away as quickly as possible, leaving them to desecrate my childhood home? Could I live with myself after that, knowing that I left my parents' home to be ransacked and God knows what else by these strangers? I pull out my phone, peering around as best as I can trying to get any visuals on the perpetrators. After confirming that I still cannot see them, I quickly open my phone and text 911, a feature that I am so thankful was enacted as law a few years ago during the pandemic.

My name is Detective Delilah Jackson. Badge number 1637. At least 2 intruders in home. I am unarmed. Send help. 1717 Relindo Drive.

I hurriedly set my phone to silent so that the incoming text message sound doesn't reverberate off the walls. Just as my finger moves off the silent button, the acknowledgment text from the 911 operator comes in. A simple "Help is on the way." I let out a silent sigh of relief, then glance up, ears straining once again to hear what the unidentified strangers are saying before firing off a text to Rita to alert her of my predicament. I slip my phone into my pocket, as the intruders round the corner of the stairwell. Their faces transform from a quick moment of shock at seeing someone else in the home to a sick look of amusement.

My blood runs cold as my gaze meets theirs. And suddenly, I place the mysterious smell that slowly wafted up the stairs a few moments ago. The new tenants from my apartment complex. *Sean and Mike, was it? What are they doing in my father's house?!*

A sneer runs across Sean's tanned face. "Well, well, well. We didn't expect to see you here, *pet*."

I stifle a gag as the pet name leaves his lips. Who was this man to think he could talk to me like that? Where did his entitlement to call me such an intimate name come from? And again—

"What the fuck are you doing in my father's house?!" That part I blurt, unintentionally, out loud.

The two men inch closer to my spot on the staircase, their chapped lips curling upward. In my haste to back away, I stumble into the step and my ankle connects with the hardwood, causing me to lose my balance. Before I hit the floor behind me, Mike shoots out his arm, grabbing the front of my shirt and pulling me to his chest. The overpowering smell of his Axe body spray is enough to make me nauseous. Instinctually my arms press out against him, trying to put distance between us. He's a lot stronger than his lanky appearance lets on. He grips my t-shirt tighter, pulling me in until his face is as close as he can get without his lips physically touching me. My stomach lurches at his close proximity and all survival instincts and police training abandon me as his breath hits my skin.

"We must stop running into each other like this," he coos into my ear, nipping my lobe slightly. I can feel my face drain of what little color it has.

"Agreed," I snarl, fighting back the urge to hurl all over this man.

Mike spins me around as if I were nothing but a rag doll and slams me into Sean's chest, the back of my head colliding with his shoulder. As if they are working in a sickening synchronization, Sean grips my biceps with his hands. Hard.

"Don't worry, *pet*," Sean growls in my ear. A shock of terror runs through my spine. "Now we can finish what we started in the laundry room."

He pins me tighter to his chest as Mike's hands begin to wander over my t-shirt. My eyes widen as I struggle against his hands. His fingertips digging into my slender arms. Sean burrows his nose into my hair, inhaling deeply. I can feel him pressing deeper into my back as Mike's hands begin to tear my shirt in a frenzy. I am completely paralyzed. Frozen in fear and time itself has stopped. Tears well up in my eyes and my throat goes dry.

This is...this is really happening.

The first tear slips silently down my sunken cheeks. Then the next. And the next. Until they're an onslaught of never-ending silent pleas for help.

Help.

Where is my help?

Where are the police?

Why are they taking so long?

Minutes tick by, feeling like an eternity. My vision blurs the scene around me to a hazy white with everything out of focus. I can no longer feel anything on or around my body. I am weightless yet stuck. How long until someone saves me? How long until they stop?

Please! Stop! Please! Mommy, make them stop!

The terrified little girl's voice rings through my head again. WHO IS SHE?! Why won't anyone save her?! Why am I the only one who knows she exists? Where can I find her? She needs help! I *need* to help her!

Mommy, please! I'll be good! Mommy, please! It hurts, Mommy! Make them stop! I don't want to! Mommy, please! Someone save me! Please!

Pain tears through my heart listening to this phantom of a girl that no one seems to be able to hear or see.

I hear you, little one. And I will find you. I will save you.

CHAPTER NINETEEN

Sirens. Flashing red and blue lights. Flashlights shining in my eyes. I can slowly make out the silhouettes of people wandering my parents' home looking for the intruders I messaged about. But they're no longer here. They left long before help ever arrived.

"Delilah Jackson?" a deep voice calls out from somewhere in the distance. Or maybe they're right in front of me. I don't know what is going on anymore. "Delilah Jackson," they say again.

I shake my head and will my eyes to refocus on the human standing in front of me. A young cop, one I've never seen before, with sandy blond hair and the brightest green eyes I've ever seen. I glance down to where his name tag rests but I cannot seem to read it. His entire form blurs in and out of focus at random intervals and I can't make out any part of his uniform. I look back up at him, my eyes staring blankly back into his. Or, at least, where I presume his face is.

"Delilah, my name is Officer Lee. Can you tell me what happened?"

"What...happened?" I repeat softly. What *did* happen? Everything feels like an endless nightmare. Is it even the same day? The sky is darker outside than it was when I first got to my dads' house. How long have I been here?

"Detective Jackson, I need you to try to think really hard, okay? What happened? Do you remember why you contacted us?"

"What...?" I repeat again, the words tasting foreign on my lips. Is this what victims feel like when I interview them? Or even witnesses? Am I also this pushy? It's truly no wonder why some of them snap during those conversations. Having to dredge up memories that your brain is blocking you from accessing is one of the most tiring things I have ever experienced.

"Delilah?! Delilah, where are you?!" I hear a familiar voice calling my name from somewhere behind Officer Lee. "Let me through, *tu hijo de puta*! That's my partner!" Her dark-brown eyes blaze as I watch her animated frame square up against the line of cops at the door.

Rita! But why...? Realization dawns on me as quickly. My text from earlier. She...she actually came. To save *me*?

Rita, in all of her five-foot nothingness, barges past the officers congregating in the doorway, their shouts from behind her bouncing off the walls. She really is a force to be reckoned with when she's on a mission to get what she wants. I guess that's why she was always the "bad cop" whenever we have to interrogate a suspect. Despite her rough exterior, I have seen Rita take a softer tone when it comes to talking with victims of sexual assault or children who have witnessed horrific events. Everyone else is fair game for her gruff attitude, though.

Her dark-tan hands gently grip my shoulders as she squats in front of me. "Hey..."

I stare blankly at her. Her face is the only thing in the room that has a definitive shape. My brain is still hazy on anything that has happened and I can't seem to form any coherent sentences. My hair falls into my face as my body begins to involuntarily tremble. I can feel tears start to prick my eyes and I begin to panic. I can't have Rita or the other officers see me crumble. I'm already a pariah for my OCD, I don't need to be one for having a breakdown, too.

"Delilah...Delilah, what's wrong? What happened?" Rita cups my cold cheeks in her hands and surveys my face. Worry lines begin to work their way across her furrowed brow. By the look on her face, she knows what happened, even if my brain is failing to form the words that I need to say. We have seen these cases before. The distant stares, the inability to recall recent events or to even find one's voice. But Rita's gentle tone and demeanor are enough for me to figure out what my brain is currently forcing me to forget.

The tears start to trickle out of the corner of my eyes and I curse myself for not being able to hold them back. I drop my chin to my chest and sob uncontrollably. The tremors raking over my body in strong waves. I clench my eyes closed as tight as I can, fighting an internal monologue that no one can hear. I feel Rita's hands gently tilt my chin upward so she can look at my face. Like a child being scolded, I rip my head out of her hands and try to focus on something beyond her and the officers dusting for prints around the living area.

"Delilah, focus. I need you to focus." Rita's words are firm yet still softly spoken, an air to her voice that I have never heard her use before when speaking to me. It causes me to panic even more instead of soothing me like she hopes. Rita shifts her focus to the officers behind her and their words start to sound like the adults in Peanuts. The *whamp whamp whamp* reverberating in my ears.

And suddenly, I'm drowning.

My body feels like it's vibrating and my skin is crawling. I swear I can feel tiny bugs skittering across my thin arms and I start to claw at my skin trying to get rid of the irritating feeling.

"I...I..." I start to stammer.

Rita and the officers heads' whip back in my direction at the first words I've spoken in what feels like hours but it was probably only ten minutes or so.

"Que pasa?" Rita tilts her head at me.

I begin to quickly glance around my dad's house and even back up the stairs that I have been sitting on since Sean and Mike...

No. That didn't happen. Things like this just *don't* happen to cops. We stop the bad guys from doing these things. These things just *don't* happen to those of us meant to protect and seek justice for everyone else. I can feel heat start to creep up my face and sweat form on my forehead. My heart beats hard in my rib cage and a tinny ringing permeates my thoughts, causing my head to start throbbing. I launch myself off the stairs, nearly knocking my partner to the ground in my haste to stand.

"I..." I repeat a stammer again, everyone's eyes bearing into me. I begin to sway.

Rita jumps up and makes a grab for me. "Delilah! You need to take it easy."

"No!" I bite out a little harshly. I move out of her reach and take a few uneasy steps toward the door and the gaggle of officers. "I...I'm...o...kay..."

My words start to trail off as I stumble on my legs like a newborn deer and suddenly I'm falling as the world fades to black.

My head is pulsating and I feel something soft underneath me. I slowly open my eyes to take in my surroundings. Creamy yellow walls, itchy linens, and a distinct disinfectant smell. A...hospital? I make an attempt to sit up only to be met with a sharp pain in my head and a cool hand pressing onto my shoulder.

"Hey..." It's Rita. Did she bring me here? What happened?

"What...what's going on?" My throat is dry and my voice sounds thick. I feel like I have been hit by a truck.

"You passed out. Those *pendejos* from the other precinct kept badgering you about what happened. You stood up, trying to speak and well..."

She trails off, looking in the other direction. Looking at anything other than me. I have never seen her like this in all the time we have worked together. To see my partner, who is usually so stoic and hardened to harsh world around us, unable to grasp at words unsettles me.

The beeps fill my ears, getting louder and louder with each shrill announcement of their presence. Rita's words—or lack thereof—bounce around in my brain, trying to connect the dots to make sense of it all. And then it hits me like a ton of bricks. The sound of the little girl screaming for help joining the cacophony of noise in my head. My heart quickens as I start to recall what happened on those stairs. Their hands all over my exposed skin. Clawing and biting and digging their fingertips into my pale flesh. Yanking my shirt up above my head and their mouths roaming to places that I did not consent to.

The world is spinning again and I can feel the hot burn of stomach acid creeping up my throat. I feel my face pale and suddenly I am leaning over the edge of the hospital bed projectile vomiting what little sustenance I have in my body all over the yellowing hospital floor. By the time I am done emptying the contents of my stomach, my abdomen screams in agony and I am panting. My body convulses in the aftershock of the emesis, my head aches even more than it did before, and the burning sensation still coats my throat.

In my upheaval, Rita must've slipped out to grab a nurse because by the time I flop myself backward onto the uncomfortable bed, she is escorting them into my room. The entire floor on the right side of my bed is coated in thick yellow-green stomach bile. I watch as the nurse's face wrinkles in disgust before it quickly switches to a look of compassion.

"Well, then...I guess we'll need a mop," she says as she saunters back out of the room, closing the door behind her.

Rita's face softens as she pulls a chair closer to the vomit-free side of my bed. We sit in an uncomfortable silence with only the sound of the heart monitor and its steady beeping to break up the quiet. I close my eyes and sink back into the stiff hospital pillow, fighting back tears of the memory of my last trip to a hospital.

Dad.

The last time I ever saw my dad, he was seizing and coughing up blood. The scene plays out again in my memory as if I am watching some horrific television show that is repeating on every channel. A memory I will never escape from. I clench my eyes tight and press my palms into them, struggling to stop the tears from forming. But it doesn't help. I can feel the hot streaks forcing their way out from the corners of my eyes as I stifle a sob.

A gentle hand touches the top of my head, almost tentatively, before smoothing out my disheveled hair. I can hear whispers coming from Rita, almost as if she's humming. No, singing? Is Rita...singing to me? I strain my ears to try and make out the words.

"...la luna vino a preguntar. Si estas dormido. Para poderte iluminar y soñar contigo..."

"I didn't know you could sing," I murmur softly, keeping my eyes closed.

"Mi madre used to sing it to me when I was little. It always made me feel better and you look like you could use some cheering up." She withdraws her hand off the top of my head. "Or something," she adds quickly.

The uncomfortable silence is back but I can still feel her standing by my bedside. After a few more long minutes of silence, I sigh and open my eyes to look at her.

"I thought you hated me," I say bluntly.

A look of shock washes over her face. "Qué?"

"I thought you hated me, just like everyone else in the precinct," I repeat myself, somewhat surprised by her confusion.

"What ever gave you that idea?!" She almost sounds affronted.

"I don't know," I admit bashfully. "Maybe it's the way you look at me with my compulsions or just your overall demeanor, especially when Jimmy is around and—"

"Stop. Stop. Stop," Rita interjects. "Delilah, I wouldn't exactly call us *besties*, but that doesn't mean I *hate* you."

I look away, admittedly ashamed. Rita has never treated me like shit like Jimmy or any of his cohorts. She has also never shown this level of care toward me before either. I'm not sure how to take the news that she doesn't hate me. I so thoroughly instilled the idea into my own head that it has become a reality for me that I've lived with since we became partners. So, rather than responding, I just give a single nod and stare at the ceiling tiles again.

"I *do* care about you, Delilah. I'm sorry if I ever made you think that I hated you. And, for what it's worth," she continues, "I *am* sorry."

I turn my head to look at her again, blinking in confusion. "Sorry? For what?"

"Your dad, mostly. I know he meant the world to you. He was a great man. I'm proud I get to work with his daughter." She smiles then sighs, looking downward. "But I'm also sorry that I took so long to get to you yesterday."

Now it was my turn to cut her off. "Don't do that."

"Do what?" She cocks her head inquisitively.

"Don't blame yourself for what happened." We have done this same song and dance with many victims and witnesses before. It is odd having to say it to her. I guess you never really know how you would handle a situation until you're actually in it. Hell, I didn't think I would turn into a scared child any time I saw those men. A shudder runs down my spine at the thought of Sean and Mike and their roaming hands.

We fall back into silence as Rita sits back in her chair, playing on her phone. It's reassuring to know she doesn't hate me, so I guess that's one weight off of my shoulders. But I am still left wondering about the events of the day before with no one able to give me answers to those questions. Answers that I'm not even sure I want.

CHAPTER TWENTY

A soft knock on my hospital room door breaks up the now comfort-able silence that has permeated the space. Rita has nodded off in the chair beside my bed, and I am still shocked that she has even stayed this long. Her words "*I wouldn't exactly call us besties but that doesn't mean I hate you*" are bouncing around in my head. No, I never would've pinned us for "besties" but I truly thought she hated me. Having confirmation that she doesn't slightly lessens the grief around my heart of feeling utterly alone. Even if our comradery is just because of our status at work.

"Yes?" I call in response to whoever knocked, but the door is already slowly opening. Why do they even bother knocking when they're not going to wait for a response before they open the door? The increasing urge to leap out of this bed, leads and all, to fiddle with the lock surges through me. I am very quickly overcome with a sense of being unsafe. Something that won't be made right until I lock and unlock the door repeatedly until the nagging itch in my core subsides.

"Detective Jackson?" a gentle voice responds back as they shut the door behind them with a soft *click*. "I'm Doctor Mathias. I just came in to check on how you were feeling today and to go over test results."

"Test results?!" I blurt out a little too loudly, startling Rita awake.

The doctor jerks his head toward Rita as if he wasn't expecting some-one to be in the room with me. "Oh! Detective Hernandez, I didn't realize you would still be here."

I shoot a quizzical glance in Rita's direction and she frowns. "I had a rape kit and STI test done on you, Del."

Del. In the entire decade we've been partnered up, she has never used a nickname for me before. She has always called me by my last name. Or, more frequently, nothing at all. More like she was always talking to air and I just so happened to be there. When did she get so...so *mushy*?! Her unusually soft demeanor in comparison to her tough, hardened exterior is a bit harder to adjust to than I would have anticipated. It could also just be because I'm so used to the "bad cop" persona that seeing her any other way just feels like I'm in a parallel dimension. Is this her way of trying to become *friendly*? Or to mitigate the severity of what was just spoken? Whatever was going on with her, it just felt *wrong*.

"...son? Detective Jackson?" My name echoes among the beeping monitors and I'm brought out of my thoughts on Rita's odd behavior.

"S-sorry," I whisper. "I think I blanked out for a minute. What did you say?"

"Detective Jackson, Detective Hernandez called an ambulance for you after you passed out during your interview," Doctor Mathias starts, looking between Rita and me as if wondering how much he should or *could* share. "Detective Hernandez informed us that you may have been sexually assaulted before the police arrived, so she requested a rape kit be performed."

"WHILE I WAS PASSED THE FUCK OUT?!" I see red. How *dare* they test me without my consent! How *dare* they think that that is even okay?! "HOW DARE YOU EVEN THINK TO TOUCH ME WITHOUT ME SIGNING SOME SORT OF CONSENT FORM?! SHE DOESN'T SPEAK FOR ME!" My words spew like venom at Rita. So *this* is why she was being all nicey-nice to me, because she broke protocol. She broke the *law* and wanted to butter me up so I wouldn't do what I'm doing right now: causing a scene. A loud whining noise echoes in my ear, causing pain to pulsate behind my eyes.

Doctor Mathias arches one of his perfectly groomed eyebrows at me and steals a sideways glance at Rita, who has worry written across her face.

"Do you not remember?"

Despite their voices being on two different octaves, the rage and high pitch whine resounding through my brain makes it hard to discern who is speaking. My surroundings blur as white hot rage courses through the rest of my body. My brain's protective shields seem to drop as the lines of reality now and reality then start to blur. I can *see* them. I can *smell* them. I can *feel* them. Their hands groping at places they didn't belong. I shake my head furiously.

"NO I DON'T REMEMBER WHAT HAPPENED IN THAT HOUSE!" I start to claw at the sticky EKG leads on my chest, ripping bits of flesh in the process. The tiny electrodes begin to feel like branding irons against my skin. "GET THESE THINGS OFF OF ME!"

I am losing my temper and I can't stop myself. I need the wires and all of this tape off. I need this IV out. I need out!

Rita grabs my hand firmly and pulls it away from where I am clawing at my chest. "Do you not remember signing the papers? We talked about this as soon as we got here."

I look at her, trying to understand what she just said, "What?" The words come out harsher than intended, but I just can't seem to wrangle in my emotions.

"We *did* get your consent. You honestly didn't say much but you were cognizant and signed all the papers needed." Rita drops my hand and reaches for the papers that are piled on the bedside table. She shoves them into my hands, her hardened demeanor back.

I glower up at her and the doctor as I sift through the pages. My expression softens to embarrassment as I see my signature at the bottom of the crisp white page. *Delilah Jackson.*

"I..." My face flushes crimson as I struggle to find the words to explain how I don't remember signing this paper or even having the kit done. How could I just forget something so invasive as a rape kit? I've seen how the steps are done in previous cases, so how did I not remember any of that being done to me? How could I have so easily forgotten the flashing of the cameras photographing every imperfect inch of my skin, the cold gloves poking and prodding me in places they shouldn't be? The swabs in my most intimate of places. The never ending questions on the whos and wheres.

My face must be panic-stricken, because the doctor's voice softens as he speaks.

"It's all right. Anger and loss of time or even memory are common when you go through a traumatic event," he reassures. There is a long pause between us before he opens the folder he's been carrying. "Are you comfortable with me relaying these results with Detective Hernandez in the room?" I nod absentmindedly.

He continues, "I am glad to tell you that all tests for sexually transmitted diseases or infections came back negative. We sent out the samples to a lab to check for anything we couldn't test for in-house. I still recommend taking antivirals just as a precaution. As far as physical examination, we did find abrasions around your bikini line and bruising on your thighs. We sent all DNA swabs and photos off to a specialty lab for further processing."

The doctor's words begin to trail off but I can see his mouth is still moving. However, everything else around me is as if someone hit the "mute" button on the world. For all intents and purposes, not finding any physical trauma to my vagina is a good thing; my body hasn't been violated in the most heinous manner. At least, not that they could see. Or, maybe the more correct phrasing would be: not that they're telling me. *God, when did I become so cynical and untrusting of people in authority?* Every intimate part of me feels like it is on fire. I wonder if this, too, is this normal. What about losing huge chunks of time *before* this incident? What qualifies as trauma?

I wish I knew what my brain is trying to protect me from. Why can I remember my life only from when Mom and Dad adopted me? What was my life like for the thirteen years prior? If only someone would've told me why my birth parents gave me up so late in life, then I wouldn't have to sit her and wonder. But now, with both sets of my parents dead, that knowledge has died with them. At the realization of this, my heart drops and I begin to sob uncontrollably again. What has my life turned into? I have never cried so much before in my life and now I just can't seem to stop.

I remember, shortly after I was adopted, my parents took me to therapy. Something about it being standard protocol to help adopted children "deal with" something so great and potentially triggering—or, at least, that's what they told me. I saw a therapist for about six months and during that time, the only thing she ever reported on was my obsession with locking things, but otherwise, apparently I was "emotionally sound" for being thirteen.

So when did I become such a mental mess?

"This is all just standard protocol, Detective Jackson. I understand how scary this all can be," the doctor says, making a poor attempt to console me. But it's all in vain as he's consoling me for the wrong reasons. Nothing anyone says can make my heart any less heavy. My entire world has been ripped away from me. First my mom when I was just sixteen and now almost twenty years later, my dad has left this earth, too. I was not given enough time with either of my parents, and now I need to try and manage this life without them. When did I become so dependent on having my parents? I guess that's probably a dumb question. Nobody can really prepare for the aftermath of losing one parent, let alone two.

"I need to go home," I manage to choke out in between sobs.

"Pardon?"

"I need to go home," I repeat again, this time a little louder, sniffling.

"Detective Jackson, I don't think that's wise. We want to run some more tests to make sure you're safe to go home. Passing out—"

"I NEED TO GO HOME!" I yell through the tears.

"Jackson," Rita snaps at me. "Calm the fuck down. You're not going anywhere."

I whirl my head toward Rita, glaring at her. "No! I *am* going home! And no one is going to stop me!" I, once again, begin ripping at the leads that are still stuck to my body. Tiny prickles of blood pool on top of my skin where the leads used to sit.

"Detective Jackson, please stop. If you want to leave against medical advice—"

"The hell you can't!" Rita whirls on the doctor. "She needs to stay and be treated!"

"Detective Hernandez, unfortunately, Detective Jackson is an adult and not under any sort of hold that would legally allow me to keep her here." Doctor Mathias turns his attention back to me, his face hard. "Detective

Jackson, while I do feel it is in your best interest to stay, I can't hold you here. But I will need you to sign some paperwork stating that you are going against medical advice."

I begin to feel like a petulant child fighting against anyone who will listen. I honestly should just stay for testing to see what caused me to pass out, but my fear of them either catching onto my disordered eating and throwing me into rehab or throwing me into the psychiatric ward for my multiple breakdowns just within the last hour alone is enough to make me want to refuse any help. My skin is crawling and I do not feel safe within these four walls. I need to be able to lock all the doors and windows three times each. Only then will I be safe. Only then will my heart stop pounding in my ears and my nerves stop feeling like they're being lit on fire. Only then will it finally feel like the world isn't burning down around me.

CHAPTER TWENTY ONE

VICTIM #3

Night has settled over the city like a thick, inky shroud. The low light of the apartment building combined with the faint glow of the crescent moon creates an ominous ambiance in the courtyard. The terracotta-colored stucco walls are darkened by shadows, and the hallway lights, suspended from the ceiling at regular intervals, flicker sporadically one after the other, as if they are engaged in a silent conversation with the unseen forces that linger in the atmosphere. The buzzing hum accompanying the erratic illumination adds an eerie undertone to the otherwise hushed environment.

Abruptly, the tranquility of the apartment complex is shattered by an incessant knocking that echoes through the still courtyard. The residents inside apartment 143 glance at the clock; it is well past midnight. Who it could possibly be that feels the need to be so obnoxious to get their attention and why they can't wait until the morning, the occupants are unsure. The knocks persist, growing louder and more urgent with each passing moment, adding to the inhabitants amplifying frustration at the intrusion to their otherwise quiet night of beer and video games.

Gruffly, the younger of the two roommates tosses his controller onto the coffee table next to him. Expletives permeate the air through gritted teeth as he stomps the ten feet from his cracked La-Z-Boy of varying shades of brown to the door.

"Yeah!? Who is it?! What do you want?!" The dirty blond-haired man slams his palm against the door jamb as he presses his face against the peep hole. Through the distorted lens, he can discern little more than the silhouette of a person standing outside the door. The hallway lights continue to flicker intermittently, casting an eerie glow that accentuates the mystery surrounding the visitor.

As the knocks continue, a very drunk Mike is becoming increasingly more disgruntled, slurring incoherently at the disturbance at his door so late at night.

He yanks open the door, nearly toppling backwards with the force. "What the fuck do you—" he stops short as he's greeted with a figure clad all in black. His scowl morphs into a sinister smile, almost as if he was trying to be sincere but failing miserably. Mike leans against the door frame, the mix of overused Axe body spray, cheap beer, and body odor wafting from him and assaulting the visitor's nostrils.

"Well, well, look who decided to come pay us a visit, Sean." Mike looks over his shoulder back at his roommate. Sean stops rage smashing the worn out buttons on the XBOX controller to peer over the back of the recliner. His cracked lips turn upward into what is supposed to be some sort of friendly grin, but it just reminds the outsider of a prepubescent boy trying too hard to imitate the debonair men of the movies.

Silence hangs in the air between the occupants of the apartment and their unannounced visitor, broken only by the erratic buzz of the flickering lights. The mysterious figure remains silent, a foreboding presence outside the door. The minutes stretch like taffy as the blackened figure waits to be invited in.

"Don't just stand there." Sean's southern drawl is thicker than normal with the addition of alcohol, to the point of being barely understandable. "Yer letting all the cold air out. Come! Have a drink with us!"

That's all the black clad figure needs to hear as a sly grin snakes across their face. They step across the threshold of the apartment, cognizant of their body placement as Mike shuts and locks the door after ushering the visitor in. Mike and Sean's apartment is a chaotic configuration of mismatched furniture, scattered clothes, and the lingering scent of old takeout and an overflowing garbage can. A haphazard collage of Sports Illustrated and porn star posters adorns the walls. The only furniture in the living room is two worn out, leather La-Z-Boys and a mismatched coffee table that is covered in a plethora of empty beer bottles, condom wrappers, and overflowing ashtrays.

The state of the kitchenette isn't any better. It is evident that the garbage can hasn't been taken out in weeks, and its contents spills onto the floor. Piles of empty takeaway containers and beer bottles litter the counters. An unopened box of garbage bags sits among the clutter, the irony not lost on their current company. Unidentifiable sticky spills coat the otherwise untouched stove.

It will take a miracle for these men to get their deposit back should they ever leave.

The mysterious guest, while a good few inches shorter than either man, holds themselves with an air of confidence so thick, no one could ever guess the dark secrets that lurk beneath their cool smile. Mike stumbles from the front door to the fridge, yanking it unceremoniously open. Bending down, the very drunk man reaches into the fridge—which appears to be just as dirty as the rest of the apartment—grabbing three cold beers.

Scratching his ass with the hand holding two of the beer bottles, Mike holds the single bottle out to his house guest. "Beer?"

The outsider shakes their head, tucking a strand of hair that has come loose back into their cap. Mike scoffs. "Suit yerself. Sean!?"

The older of the two men looks over and reaches for the outstretched beverage, twisting the cap off in one fell swoop. The visitor wrinkles their nose as the older of the two men takes a giant swig from the glass bottle that was just rubbing against his roommates—probably unclean—ass. Mike stumbles over to his original position on the La-Z-Boy and plops down onto it, the furniture creaking under his weight. The worn out chair has definitely seen better days long before it ever entered into this dirty bachelor pad. Hints of spilled beer and various snack crumbs have left their mark, embedded into the various splits in the leather. The reclining mechanism, though slightly strained, still manages to extend with an audible groan. It's considered a "good day" if the men don't have to fight to get the chair to recline. The cushions, once plump and inviting, have succumbed to the inevitable sag of prolonged use.

The armrests tell a story of their own, bearing the indents of countless arms and faint ring marks from occasionally being used as makeshift coasters. Faded patches suggest spots where spilled drinks were hastily wiped away or, more often than not, left behind until they dried onto the upholstery, leaving behind crusty dark spots. Remnants of remote control battle scars and game controller imprints adorn the armrests, evidence of countless hours lost in virtual worlds.

The interloper shifts from one foot to the other, adjusting their black duffle bag on their shoulder. Whatever is in the bag must be heavy and weighing on them. However, despite the heft of its contents, its owner never lets the bag leave their side.

Sean looks up from the video games he has been sucked into and stares at the newcomer, his eyes glassy from the alcohol and the prolonged staring at the television screen.

"Aren't you going to sit?" His words are still nearly incomprehensible. The smell of beer radiates off of him from his position on the chair to the spot where the figure stands.

"Where?" the visitor sneers, uttering their first words since crossing the threshold into the foul apartment. "It's either your lap or *his* lap and frankly, I'd rather not."

"Whatever." Sean rolls his eyes and throws back the remaining contents of his drink. "Go be of some use and grab Mike and me another round...and get yerself something to drink. If you're going to hang out with us, you need to at least loosen up."

The guest glares at both men but walks over to the cluttered kitchen anyway. Executing their plan is going to be easy now that the men are having them grab drinks. There won't be any need for convincing if they're this willing to accept drinks from a virtual stranger. Sliding their hand into the side pocket of their duffle bag, they pull out two black disposable gloves and slip them on before carefully pulling on the sticky refrigerator door handle. The seal on the refrigerator door releases with a loud squelching noise. The figure grimaces at the sound and general uncleanliness of the apartment.

Setting the glass bottles on the only clear counter space available, the uninvited guest slides their gloved hand into their bag, fishing around for their item of choice. They flip a small Ziplock bag filled with white powder in between their fingers, an amused smile playing on their lips. Their eyes fixate on the back of the unsuspecting men's heads as the figure absent-mindedly opens the baggy and empties a little bit of the contents into each beer bottle. They swirl the bottles slightly to help incorporate the white powder throughout the liquid. Quietly, the guest-turned-barmaid saunters over to the residents of the apartment—both of whom are still engrossed in their video games—and nonchalantly holds the drinks out. Without saying thank you, both men snatch the cold bottles out of their hands and take giant swigs.

The visitor stands silently in front of the men, watching their faces intently, hoping they don't taste anything extra added to their drinks.

"Well don't just stand there!" Sean hollers. "Sit yer ass down and enjoy yourself!"

The interloper cringes and hopes the men don't notice. They need to make the bachelors believe that they're willing to do whatever is asked of them for their plan to work. Looking around the room, they attempt to figure out where they're supposed to sit or "relax" that doesn't involve touching any filthy part of the apartment. Cautiously, they clear a spot on the coffee table and try to hover just slightly above the surface so as to not get any of the sticky substances on their clothing.

Twenty minutes go by and Sean and Mike have completely finished their beers. Their eyes are drooping slightly more than they were before. Mike burps and sways in his chair.

"I, *uh*, I need another." Mike tries to push himself out of the chair, falling backward into it.

"No worries. I got it." The visitor quickly gets up from their spot on the coffee table, snagging both empty beer bottles.

"Yew dun need ta trow...away..." Sean slurs, his cheeks flushed red.

They shake their head. "It's no problem. Just stay put and I'll bring you your beers."

Once in the kitchen, they quickly recreate the beer and powder mixture they made twenty minutes ago. Everything is going according to plan. Back in the living room, both men have begun sweating, panting, and murmuring to themselves.

With as much fake concern as they can muster, the intruder saccharinely coos, "Are you okay? You don't look so hot. Here," they thrust the beers at Mike and Sean, "drink something cold."

Mike and Sean chug the cold, spiked liquid in one motion in an effort to cool off from the heat wave that begins to creep from their groin up to their throat. Sean grabs the front of his shirt, pulling it back and forth in an attempt to circulate air around his torso.

"Fuuuuuck," Sean moans, pulling his shirt off. "Mike...Mike. MIKE!"

A soft sound of acknowledgment leaves Mike's throat as he, glassy-eyed, stares at his roommate. Mike starts running his hands over the bulge forming in his pants, breathing heavily. He moves his limbs as quickly as is possible in his inebriated state and leans over to grab the remote. Almost as if he cannot get to his preferred program fast enough, as soon as Mike finds a channel playing pornography, he yanks his stiffening cock out of his gym shorts.

This is working quicker than I expected. The mysterious visitor smirks to themselves as both men, oblivious to the guest still in their home, begin to pleasure themselves to the women on the television.

Slightly disgusted and dumbfounded that one, these men would masturbate in front of each other, and two, it was like they had completely forgotten they had someone else in their home, the now very uncomfortable guest turns their back to the men. They take a few deep breaths and remember they have a mission to complete and the world would not be safe until it was finished.

Sucking in a deep breath, the stealthy houseguest heads toward one of the open doors, shouldering their duffle bag in the process. "Hey, Mike?" they call out.

Mike grunts in response through a panting breath. Thankfully neither men are focused on their visitor, or they would have seen their entire face twist into a very visible cringe.

Clearing their throat loudly, the outsider tries again to get the heated man's attention. "Can I talk to you...Alone?"

The blond man glances over his shoulder and spots the interloper standing by the bedroom door. His eyes light up as he shoves himself back into his shorts, staggering as he jumps out of the chair. The alcohol and mysterious powder the visitor poured into their beers has finally hit him. Wobbling on his feet, Mike makes the arduous walk from his recliner to the bedroom that is only five feet away.

The visitor shuts the bedroom door and locks it behind them as soon as Mike is past the threshold. Before he has a chance to turn around, a slimy smirk already plastering his face, the interloper slings a rope around his neck, dead-weighting themselves downward to choke out the taller man. The mix of alcohol and drugs makes it quite easy for them to overtake the man, despite his much larger size. As Mike's heavy body starts to slump into unconsciousness, the black-clad figure hurriedly maneuvers his body to the bed, using what little strength Mike has left to their advantage. The incapacitated man lands on his dingy mattress with a deafening thud. Thankfully, the drug-laced beer seems to have been enough to keep Sean pretty stationary while the assailant takes care of Mike.

Reaching into the duffle bag, they pull out a thick, black, plastic tarp, fighting to get it underneath the unconscious man on the bed. They would have to be quick as Mike could wake up any minute and if he's not fastened in place, it could ruin the whole plan. Once the tarp is secured under him, the invader quickly grabs the restraints and gags out of their bag and ties the helpless man up.

While waiting for Mike to come to, the attacker continues to set up the tools of their trade: an eight inch dildo and various razor blades and sharp knives. The last piece of this plan is a Bluetooth speaker hooked up to the invader's phone to blare music as loud as possible to drown out any screams that are about to ensue.

And there will be screaming. The assailant relishes in.

Ten minutes pass and Mike isn't showing any sign of regaining consciousness. The attacker huffs out an exasperated sigh and saunters over to check on the pulse of the passed out man.

Still breathing. Just knocked out.

This won't do. There is still so much left in the plan that needs to be accomplished before daybreak and it is nearing closer and closer. Frustrated that this man is not rising, the visitor smacks Mike across the cheek as hard as they can.

Nothing.

Whatever. They'll have to start the process even if he's asleep. It just means that the screams of this sick bastard will be a bit delayed, is all.

Like an artist admiring their materials, the attacker eyes their implements of torture with an intense passion. The thought of using each and every device sends shivers of delight up their spine. They have been envisioning this moment their entire life, and it is finally judgment day.

Selecting a thin, sharp razor blade, the invader traces it along Mike's jaw with just enough pressure to cause a thin bead of blood to trail behind it. Mike begins to stir beneath a light moan of pain. A wicked smile creeps across the assailant's chapped lips. It is time.

"Good morning, princess," they chortle, mocking the weary man.

"What the—?!"

Mike's words are quickly hushed as the attacker presses the razor blade to his lips. "Shh, shh, shh. No one wants to hear your whining and pleading."

The helpless man's bloodshot eyes widen as he tries to focus on his attacker's face. Despite his best efforts, Mike is still too intoxicated to be able to keep his eyes open for more than a few moments. Another quick cut with the razor blade across Mike's jawline is enough to force his eyes open as he sucks in a breath of pain.

The assailant tuts in disapproval. "Now, now, Mike. Is this how you accept your punishment? Do try to keep your eyes open or it'll only be worse."

"What the fuck do you think you're doing, you sick *fuck*?!" Mike spits out the last word as if it alone is enough to stop the assault on his body.

The enemy quickly shoves four of their gloved fingers deep into Mike's mouth, causing him to choke and sputter against the latex. "Now, now, do I need to teach you a lesson on doing as you're told or are you going to shut. The fuck. Up." The attacker spits out their sentence in a sharp staccato, shoving their fingers deeper into Mike's throat with each annunciation.

Tears form in the tied up man's eyes as he gags around the latex-covered fingers of his attacker. As the adversary pulls their fingers from Mike's salivating throat, they tap his cheek condescendingly, spittle sticking to his dirty blond stubble.

A menacing smile plays at the corner of their lips as the helpless man glowers at them. "That's a good boy. Don't worry. It'll only hurt for a minute or two."

CHAPTER TWENTY TWO

VICTIM #4

The bachelor pad is eerily quiet, save for the thunderous bass booming from the other room, rattling the walls. Mike and the visitor have been missing in action for at least thirty minutes and in Sean's drunken stupor, he almost forgot there was someone else in the apartment. *Almost.* The muffled screams that emanate from the closed door over the music behind him snap him out of his inebriated state.

"Mike?!" Sean hollers, his raspy voice slurring.

No answer.

"*Miiike!*" the drunkard hollers even louder, tumbling out of his chair.

The dark brown-haired man staggers from his position on the faded La-Z-Boy toward the closed bedroom door. The closer he gets, the more distinct the sounds coming from the other side of his roommate's door become. The screams—while slightly muted by the sounds of a thumping bass—are raw, desperate, and laced with an undeniable sense of anguish. Sean stares blankly at the barrier between him and the other two adults. The muffled grunting and bed springs creaking on the other side of the door cause Sean to cock his head in curiosity. He can't shake the feeling that something terrible is unfolding on the other side of that door. Something he isn't sure if he wants to be a part of or run away from.

He starts to debate on whether or not he should intervene, his hand hesitating inches away from the doorknob. As the minutes stretch on, the intensity of the screams ebb and flow, creating an unsettling medley of distress. Sean's concern for his friend begins to deepen, a knot tightening in his stomach. Unable to ignore the escalating unease, he finally musters the courage to knock on the door.

No response.

He knocks again, louder this time, his anxiety mounting with each unanswered rap against the wood. The silence that follows his repeated knocks starts to sober Sean up quickly as he begins to fear for his roommate. He takes a step back, contemplating his next move.

Summoning his resolve, he calls out, "Is everything okay in there? I heard screams. Do you need help?" The words hang in the air, a desperate plea for some reassurance. Sean reaches for the doorknob once more but before he can grab it, the door cracks open revealing the dark abyss of the room beyond. Blinking rapidly to adjust his eyes to the inky depths in front of him, he gently pushes it the rest of the way open and steps inside.

"Mike?" he slurs out.

Sean slowly slides his body through the door jam, careful not to trip in the darkness. Loud, melodic music pulses through the room, vibrating heavily against the makeshift dresser that is pressed against the wall. A wave of unpleasant smells—iron and bodily fluids—assaults Sean's nose, causing him to gag. His head throbs with the promise of a migraine from the concoction of booze and drugs.

"Mike....?" Sean calls into the darkness hesitantly, patting the wall in a futile attempt to find the light switch. "Dude, are you okay? Look man, I ain't gonna yuck your yum, but it fucking smells in here!"

Finally finding the plastic light switch, Sean flips it in an attempt to help illuminate the now quiet man's room. Nothing. Like a child with too much enthusiasm, he flicks the switch rapidly multiple times in an exhaustive effort to bring light to the room. All endeavors to try and make the light work are in vain. He digs through his gym shorts pocket, fishing for his phone with a sense of urgency, fingers fumbling in the confined space as he tries to grasp the elusive device. Still slightly inebriated, Sean squints in the darkness, attempting to locate the flashlight feature on his phone. His thumb dances over the screen, brushing against various icons in a clumsy, drunken quest for illumination. The faint glow from the screen briefly illuminates his determined expression.

Desperation flits across Sean's face as he continues to try and call for his friend and the stranger, both of whom are now oddly quiet. In his intoxicated state, the phone slips from his grasp. An unceremonious *"fuck!"* escapes his lips. Time seems to slow as it plummets to the ground, and Sean commits a series of clumsy reflexive movements in an attempt to catch it before it hits the carpet. The room sinks back into an inky darkness as the light from the screen disappears when the phone lands face down on the floor. Frustrated, Sean bends down to retrieve the fallen device, hoping it has survived its unintended descent.

A groan from the other side of the room, barely audible over the music, makes Sean snap his head up, and he whirls in the direction from which the sound came. The sudden noise causes Sean to forget his quest to find the flashlight on his phone, which he subconsciously shoves back into his pocket.

"Mike? Mike, what the fuck man?!" Sean pads his way in the dark toward where his muscle memory knows the bed should be. "Why the fuck isn't your light working? And why the *fuck* does it SMELL in here?!"

The scent of iron, sweat, and fear permeate every surface in the tiny apartment bedroom. Sean extends his arms trepidatiously into the impenetrable darkness, fingers outstretched like tentative antennae. His hands sweep through the void, encountering cool surfaces and the occasional unknown object covered in who knows what. After a moment that feels like an eternity, his fingertips brush against something softer and more familiar. As Sean's hands explore the bed in an attempt to find his roommate, it encounters an unexpected, warm, and squishy sensation. A sudden dread envelops him as he realizes that he hasn't found the bed linen, but rather a garbage bag laying on the bed like a sheet.

Sean lets out an involuntary *ugh* as he yanks his hand away from the unidentified liquid. A shiver runs down his spine, a mixture of surprise and disgust contorting his features. The realization of the unpleasant encounter lingers, leaving him momentarily frozen in the dark, reconsidering his next move with heightened caution. With his dry hand, he grabs his phone back out of his pocket and hastily finds the flashlight app.

In a moment of triumph, the soft glow emanates from the device, cutting through the oppressive darkness like a beacon. The narrow beam of light reveals a small portion of the room, unveiling a world that was concealed just moments ago.

The light skitters across the walls, casting long shadows that seem to retreat into the corners. Dust particles hang in the illuminated air, caught in the spotlight like ethereal fireflies. The room, once an impenetrable abyss, now takes on a new identity.

Various pieces of furniture emerge from the shadows, their outlines becoming more discernible. The dim glow highlights the various degrees of trash surrounding Seans feet, and the play of light and shadow create an almost haunted ambiance. Sean cautiously directs the beam to his hand, the one that touched the mysterious liquid on Mike's bed. A sense of unease creeps over him as he hesitates for a brief moment, reluctant to examine the strange substance.

"What the…? Is that—?" He directs his hand closer to his face, squinting in the dim light to unravel the mystery of the sticky mess on his hand.

As his eyes adjust, Sean's gaze focuses on the dark, viscous substance coating his palm. A moment of confusion lingers before recognition dawns. Horror sweeps across his face as he realizes that the warm stickiness is none other than *blood*.

The maroon liquid clings to his skin, leaving a trail of deep red in its wake as it begins to drip over his wrist. Sean, in a panic, rapidly moves his phone's flashlight around the bedroom.

"Mike? MIKE!"

Terror strikes the dark haired man as the light from his phone finally lands on his friend spread eagle, naked, on a black trash bag. Blood splatters every potential surface and puddles pool around Mike's hips. Sean moves the flashlight little by little, revealing the whole horrific scene in front of him. With every movement of the light down Mike's naked frame, the wounds get worse and worse, before the flashlight finally settles on Mike's groin, where Sean notices the most horrible sight he has ever seen.

MIKE WAS MISSING HIS PENIS!

"Oh my fucking God!" Sean screams, the threat of sickness escaping his throat at the sight of his roommate's mutilated body. Sean whirls around, shining the flashlight in every direction. "Where the fuck are you, you sick fuck?! What the fuck did you do?"

Fumes of anger crawl up his tan skin, tinting his cheeks and the tips of his ears, "Where the *fuck* are you?! Get out here and face me like a man!"

Without warning, a sharp pin prick hits Sean's neck, his blood-covered hand instinctively jerking up to feel the area. To his surprise, something is sticking out of his neck. As he yanks it out, he shines the flashlight on the object in his hand, revealing a hypodermic needle with the plunger pushed all the way down.

"What in the—?!" his voice instantly slurring.

"Don't worry. It'll only hurt for a minute or two," a sinister voice whispers in his ear as the world around him fades to black, his hands flailing around for purchase.

CHAPTER TWENTY-THREE

I groan as I roll away from my bedroom window, throwing my comforter over my head to block out the blazing sun. My body is stiff and the crook of my elbow is beginning to show signs of deep purple bruising from where the IVs were. The last few days have been an emotional blur and I'm glad to be in the comfort of my own home. Hopefully my life will get back to normal—or at least whatever my version of normal is—like it was before my dad passed away.

From under the safety of my covers, I fling my arm out and pat around my pillow trying to find my phone. When my hand smacks on the cool hard surface of the screen, I pull it quickly under my blanket and squint against the harshness of the glaring blue light.

MONDAY. 13:56

I bolt upright, the blankets flinging off my body.
Monday?!

No. No. No. No. Wasn't it just *Saturday* when I was released from the hospital? Where did the last two days go?! Was I really so worn out that I slept for two days straight? I don't even remember getting home. Did Rita give me a ride? That must've been it. I must've been strung out from all the medications and my body just needed to relax.

To be frank, for the first time in as far back as I can remember, I finally feel *rested.*

I sigh heavily, flopping backward into my pillows. It feels so weird to wake up for and actually feel...not tired? Well-rested? I'm not even sure how to describe this feeling. I feel so light and airy, like the weight of a million worlds was suddenly lifted off of my shoulders overnight. Or, I guess in this case, after (apparently) sleeping for two plus days in a row. Is this really what it feels like to not be running on empty? I guess experiencing two nights straight of trauma and heartache finally knocked my ass out enough that I got some solid sleep.

I wonder if this what most people feel on a day-to-day basis. I shake my head in mock humor and disbelief at the stress I had to go through in order to get a decent night's sleep. I could've done without that, Universe, but thanks I guess? I'm still on administrative leave for another few days, leaving me without much to do today. What does one do when they don't feel like they have to outrun the invisible boogeyman?

I flop back into my sheets, their silky coolness encircling me and momentarily staving off the late summer heat that's creeping through my bedroom window. For the first time since Dad died, I feel a renewed sense of calm, like I can get past whatever decided to try and destroy me not that long ago. Maybe that grief therapist isn't needed after all. I stay wrapped in the softness of my blankets and decide to catch up on some much needed reading which will easily eat up most of the day. Clicking the e-reader app on my phone, I select the first book in my queue and dive head first into a fantastic fantasy world with vampires, witches, and magic.

H ours must've passed as I click off of my e-reader app, finally finishing the book I had been putting off for weeks. A relaxed sigh leaves my body as I feel my shoulders slouch. This is...this is nice. This kind of slow-moving day where I'm not completely burnt out or constantly feeling like I am being watched is a feeling I could get used to. I really wonder what had to click to take my body out of fight or flight mode after all these years.

I take a peek at the time on my phone again.

MONDAY. 21:32

I was right, it's been several hours, and the constant nitpicking to get up and run or bike as hard as I can on my Peloton has begun to get louder and louder. I give into the call and don my sneakers. Even though I may have just outrun the nightmare of the screaming child, it doesn't seem like I am able to outrun the inner monologue around my body. I hit "Play" on the screen and begin my normal routine with the virtual instructor.

Halfway in and sweat is pouring from my body, my clothing sticking to my skin in random places. It feels great to be exercising and getting back into my usual day-to-day routine. At last, things seem to be going back to how they should be, and it's the normalcy that I have been craving so deeply. My thoughts of how my life is turning around are abruptly halted by a loud, gut wrenching scream that echoes throughout the apartment complex.

Dear Gods, no. Please do not let the voices start coming back. I plead with the Universe. Things were finally looking up. This cannot be starting all over again. I pause the workout routine and strain my ears for more sound. I hear footsteps running down the hallway and a faint sound of someone screaming, "Call the police!" An unintended sigh of relief escapes my body as I realize that, this time, the screaming is not in my head. The thought is then quickly overshadowed by another, less cheery realization: something terrible has happened in my complex.

I jump off my bike and run to open my apartment door. In my rush to get outside, I trip over two large boxes that have been placed on my doorstep. I don't remember ordering anything, but now is not the time to inspect them. I kick them inside, slamming the door behind me and rushing toward the crowd. It doesn't take long to get from my apartment to where the residents of our tiny gated complex congregate.

I begin to shove through the horde of onlookers, many crying, many covering their mouths in disbelief. Before I can even make it to the front of the crowd, I am hit with a wave of nausea as the smell of rotting garbage, decaying flesh, and blood creep up my nostrils. I pull my shirt over my mouth and nose, stifling the smell to get a better look at the scene in front of me.

A young girl, no older than nineteen, is sobbing uncontrollably into an elderly neighbor's embrace. I can hear her mumbling something between the sobs and hiccups into the old woman's shoulder about how she was just talking to the residents of the apartment on Saturday and how they were supposed to meet up tonight.

Just beyond her, through the open apartment door, I see what's causing her distress. Written in what looks dark red...paint? No. That unmistakable shade isn't like any paint I've seen before. The words "Dead Men Don't Rape" are written across the living room wall in *blood*.

I grab my phone from my pocket and dial 911, unsure if any of the bystanders have already made the call.

"911, what's your emergency?"

"This is Detective Delilah Jackson, badge number 1637. There has been a violent crime, possibly a homicide, at the Hillcrest Place Apartments off of Seventh and Washington."

"Can you see how many people were injured?"

"Not without walking into the crime scene, but it smells like decomp and from the front door, I can see a message written on the walls in what looks like blood."

"Okay, what does it say?"

I stare at the words on the wall. Their presence unfortunately confirms that this incident is connected to my case from earlier this month, as the exact phrasing of the message was never released to the public.

I swallow hard. "It says *Dead Men Don't Rape*."

The 911 operator takes a few more pieces of information and assures me that help is on the way and to not touch anything. The throng of people around the exposed apartment has grown, and I want nothing more than to shut the door and save us all from the smell wafting out of the apartment. But I know better. I know better than to touch anything without gloves. Flashing red and blue lights begin to illuminate our courtyard and the creak of the metal community gate resounds off the walls.

"Out of the way! Police!" Two familiar voices shout out over the crowd.

Oh Gods. It's Jimmy and Jules. I haven't seen them since my dad's funeral. I don't want them anywhere near my apartment, even if it is to help with this investigation. Jules is okay, but Jimmy gives me the ick and makes an unsafe situation feel even worse. There's just something about him that doesn't sit right with me. I try to sink back into the crowd as they approach but the minute Jimmy's eyes lock on mine, I know there is no escaping.

"Jackson," he says curtly.

"Doctré. Jules." I nod to each of them in response.

"Glad to see you up and about, Delilah." Jules offers a slight smile but quickly reverts back to a stony expression after Jimmy shoots him a look of contempt.

What the fuck is this guy's problem?

"Thanks, Jules. I'll be back to work in no time!" I return the smile even with Jimmy rolling his eyes.

"Well, we better get going. We have *actual* work to do. You know, since you can't keep your own complex safe," Jimmy snaps. "Better yet, how's your mental health? Get over that *locking* issue? I've been saying since the beginning you only kept your job because of your dad. You will *never* live up to him, so why don't you just do us all a favor and stop trying?"

Red hot rage creeps up my face. The audacity of this man! The gall! "Don't you *dare*—"

Jules cuts me off. "Seriously, Jimmy? Not appropriate."

Wow. That's a first. Jules has never stuck up for me before. What is happening? Am I in the twilight zone?

"Yeah well, women like *her* shouldn't..."

Jimmy continues on his prattling as I tune him out, taking note of my surroundings. I glance around at the ever-growing crowd. No matter the hour, tragedy will *always* pique people's interest, but something else—no wait, *someone* else—piques my interest.

Jericho?!

Lurking in the shadows is the man who is the closest thing I have to family left in this city. The man who scared the absolute shit out of me in my dad's attic shortly after the funeral. The man who, without a trace, disappeared after that alarming interaction. I turn on my heel and make a beeline for him.

"Where are you going, Jackson?" Jimmy sneers. "I wasn't done talking to you!" He laughs sarcastically and I can feel his eyes rolling.

"I don't answer to you. Now, do your fucking job," I call over my shoulder, not slowing my pace as I jog toward the last spot I saw Jericho. Where the fuck did he go? I catch him rounding a corner and I pick up my pace, calling after him.

"Jericho. Jericho! Jericho, stop!" I am breathless by the time I catch up to him. "What the fuck, man?!"

He wheels around, his face looking worse for wear than even when he was in the attic. The stench of liquor radiates from him. It seems like he has slipped back into old habits.

"I told you to run. You're not safe. Now they're *here.*" His voice is low and hoarse.

"*Who* is here? Why aren't I safe? Why won't you answer me!?"

"You. Aren't. Safe." Jericho enunciates every word.

"WHY? Quit with the goddamn word games!" I take a few deep breaths and speak to my friend in a calmer tone. "What is going on, Jericho? What aren't you telling me?"

"Delilah!?" My name echoes behind me. I turn in the direction of the voice and see Rita walking quickly toward me. I whip back around to continue my conversation with Jericho, but he is gone. He just *vanished.* I didn't even hear him move. A light hand touches my shoulder and I jump.

"Are you okay?"

"Ye...yeah," I stammer as I turn to face Rita. "Did you happen to see an older gentleman, kinda ragged-looking, just a moment ago?"

Rita arches her eyebrow at me. "No? I only saw you standing here. ¿Estás bien?"

"Yeah, I'm—I'm okay. What are you doing here?"

My partner blinks at me for a few seconds as if the flashing lights, crowd, and crime scene tape isn't a clear indicator. "I was called?...to the crime scene?"

I want to smack my forehead. As if that isn't the obvious answer. Of course she would still be getting calls to crime scenes even with me on leave. They wouldn't just not have her do anything because I'm not there. That's just ridiculous. Although a very large part of me is hurt that life is still going on without me, I know this is just the way the world works. It continues moving forward, even if you seem to be standing still.

I put on the best face I can, attempting to move quickly past my faux pas, and clap my hands once as if marking an end to that mishap.

"So, what do you need from me? I'm ready to come back! Let's figure out what monster has decided to land at my doorstep!"

I begin walking with a purpose toward the crime scene with Rita trailing behind me. Whether this is true confidence or I'm just getting better at faking it, I will never know, but I have a renewed sense of energy to just keep going and get back to my old life.

"What? Delilah, no," she calls after me but I don't slow my pace. Rita reaches out and grabs my wrist. "Delilah, stop. You're not working this case."

I force a laugh and continue in my original direction. "Of course I am. We work together. This is *our* case."

"No, Delilah, it's not. Dubris wanted me to tell you that you are still benched and to stay away. You're too close to the situation and this could be seen as tampering."

Only then do I stop in my tracks. "I know I'm not set to come back to work for a few days, but surely with this literally being right outside my door, Captain will make an exception." My voice cracks in desperation without my permission.

"That's exactly why he said no. Look, I know you're dying to get back out there but you *have* to stay out of it. The last two murders were connected to old case files your dad worked on and the captain is really upset that this information was never brought to him. He thinks you were intentionally hiding it from him. You need to leave this one alone until you're fit for duty again."

Never has something hit so literally close to home, and yet I am being dismissed by my own department because I am still on leave and "too close" to the situation just because my dad was involved in an old case. I am very rapidly becoming agitated at the treatment like I am a suspect by my comrades.

"Rita, you know I would never! I didn't tell anyone—"

"Look, I personally don't care. I'm just passing the message along. Now, go home." And with that, Rita storms off, leaving my mouth agape and my hopes of returning to work dashed.

Was not disclosing to the captain that these were linked to my dad that big of a fuck up? They were old cases. Why am I being treated like a misbehaving child? Rita also knew. Why isn't she being reprimanded the way I am?! I stand bewildered in the courtyard of my usually quiet apartment complex as the swarm of people finally starts to disperse.

The flashing lights of squad cars outside the gates barely filter into my apartment as I plop unceremoniously onto my couch in a huff. I can't believe I am, yet again, being prohibited from doing my job, even if I am still technically on leave. I can come back early. Hell, I *want* to come back early. These last few weeks without having work to keep my mind occupied have been unbearable.

I begin to pace back and forth in my small living room, creating a light indent in the carpet under my path. This is utterly ridiculous! They *need* me. They *need* an extra set of eyes, especially since this is my home. My safety net.

In my robotic pacing, I accidentally stumble over one of the large packages that I kicked inside my door before running out to see what the commotion was. I curse this box for the pain it has caused to shoot up my pinkie toe. Who the hell sent me a package anyway? Picking up the rather hefty box, I notice something immediately to alert me of what's inside.

My dead name and a case number.

I quickly scoop up both boxes, plopping one down next to the coffee table and placing the other gently on top of it. I drop onto the edge of my couch and stare at the box in front of me for what seems like an eternity. A sea of questions flies through my brain at rapid speed.

Who sent these, and how did they get their hands on them? And if I open them, what am I hoping to learn? What if I learn information about my past that I don't actually want to know? Why did Dad feel it necessary to hide these boxes—*evidence* boxes with my name on them—in the attic for all these years? What could he have been hiding? Does it even matter at this point if I was given an order from the captain to essentially stand down?

I get back up off the couch and continue my pacing, every so often walking toward the boxes and staring at them, then throwing my hands into the air and beginning to pace again. Rinse. Wash. Repeat. For about another two or three hours.

By now, the police have probably left the complex and the apartment should be taped off. It'll make the news tomorrow, but plenty of in-formation will be redacted until Dubris gives the all clear for Rita or Jimmy to divulge any details to the public. Even though the commotion in the courtyard has dissipated, my mind is still reeling at the obvious connection between this murder and the other two I was working on prior to being put on convalescence.

Daylight filters through the curtains of my apartment as I stir from my cramped position on the couch. At some point during my pacing, I decided to sit down and just *stare* at the box on the coffee table in an attempt to create some magical ability that would let me know what was in it and if it was worth opening. That clearly didn't work. Not that I was even convinced that it would work. That sort of stuff only happened in movies and my fantasy books, and even though my life—up until recently—has been playing out like a horror flick, I'm not that lucky.

I sigh heavily as I rub the crick in my neck and stretch myself up off of the couch. I saunter over to the kitchen for a Sprite Zero and continue my staring contest with the boxes.

They're winning.

I have been looking for these answers for so long, but now that they're sitting right in front of me, I'm having a hard time opening them. I don't know why is this so hard, Why I can't bring myself to just rip the yellowing tape off of the boxes. It's the same as ripping off a Band-Aid. It may hurt at first but once it's off, you can move on with your day and continue with life as normal.

In a huff, I flop backward onto my couch and read the label over and over again.

EVIDENCE

CASE NO. 17860 ITEM NO. 254

DATE 27 Sept 1998 TIME ______ AM/PM

PLACE San Diego

REMARKS Delilah Henderson

____

OFFICER/TECH Darius Jackson

The longer I stare at this brown cardboard box and faded label, the more I psych myself out about what could lie within. But even more so, something catches my eye that I know was not there when I found the boxes in my dad's attic.

A partial bloody handprint.

CHAPTER TWENTY FOUR

This can't be. That print must've been there from years ago and I just didn't notice it in my haste to get them out of the attic. Yeah. That must be it. Or maybe I had blood on my hand from the hospital and touched the box after leaving.

On second thought, I still don't know who sent these. Did I do it? I don't remember going to Dad's house after I was discharged, but I must have, and with all the pain killers, I'm just not able to recall everything. I probably set the boxes down outside to open the door and in my exhaustion, forgot about them. Yeah. *Yeah!* That's the only logical explanation. What other explanation could there be? Unless...

Jericho! This handprint *must* be from him! He was *somehow* in Dad's attic and no one noticed him and I keep seeing him at every crime scene! Realization dawns on me that our long-time family friend may not be the man we all thought he was. This is clearly the logical explanation. In fact, besides yesterday when he barely spoke a word to me after I caught him slinking away from the crime scene, I haven't seen him since that day he cornered me in Dads' attic!

Sitting crisscross on the floor between my coffee table and couch, I pull the box off the table and into my lap. I inhale deeply, holding my breath as I slowly peel back the layers of tape, the adhesive reluctantly relinquishing its grip. The box, now free from its restraints, exhales the scent of ages past—a mixture of paper, ink, and hopefully a discovery of a history long since lost to me. As the lid parts from the base, a soft whisper of air escapes, as if the contents were also holding their breath, waiting for this moment.

Inside, a chaotic jumble of folders and loose papers greet me, each sheet bearing the wrinkles and creases of time. Yellowing documents and case files with fading ink and faded photographs stare back at me, taunting me with secrets about my own life that I'm still not quite sure I am ready to unfold.

"There's no going back now," I speak out loud to the Universe. Of course, there is a "going back"! All I have done is pull back the tape. I haven't even touched the files. They're still securely in their home waiting to be lost and forgotten to the hands of time once more. I could—and should—just turn these boxes back over to Captain so that they can be archived properly. Curiosity is getting the best of me, however. I have waited all this time to know about my past and, now with Dad gone, I have an opportunity to learn about *why* I was given up for adoption in the first place. And how am I even connected to a police case file. What could've happened all of those years ago that caused Dad to *steal* a box of evidence and reports and stash them away in his attic for over two decades? Why didn't he just tell me about my past when I was eighteen like he promised? Why did Mom's death completely shut him off from ever telling me the truth?

I gently pick up the first manila file folder. It's time to see what has been hidden from me for all of these years. I release the breath I didn't realize I was still holding and flip open the folder. I gasp in audible horror as my eyes land on an old, worn out photo. Judging by the date at the bottom, I can't be much older than nine years old. I don't even remember this day, but clearly it was of some significance, as there are tons of files in here all stuffed to the brim. Even back then my skin was a ghostly white and I was just as thin. My curly blond hair sticks out of the sides of my head at all weird angles, mats visible in the photo. Varying degrees of bruises cover my jaw and eyes while a swollen, split lip makes me look monstrous. As horrifying as it is to see my former self in this ghastly of a state, it doesn't hit me as hard as it should. All the years on the force and seeing the worst side of human beings has hardened me to such atrocities.

I place the photo face down on my coffee table as I thumb through the remaining photographs, each one more horrific than the last. That is until I come to the photo that shows my stick-thin legs and hip bones, pink-and-white floral panties hiding my genitalia. My skin, typically pale as moonlight, bears the signs of raw, angry, and bright red burns, blistered and oozing. I instinctually touch the scarring on my bikini line, tears forming behind my lashes. I was always told this was a freak accident, but to be placed in a police dossier with miles upon miles of paperwork and forms, this has to be anything *but* an accident. I read the hospital report clipped to the photo, trying to put the puzzle pieces together.

ON SUNDAY, 27 SEPTEMBER, 1998, JUNIOR OFFICER TIMOTHY DUBRIS #279 AND LEAD OFFICER HARRY MARKS #843 WERE CALLED TO 986 IBIS ST. BY DISPATCH AT 12:17 PM WHEN A NEIGHBOR REQUESTED A WELFARE CHECK AFTER HEARING SCREAMS COMING FROM THE HOME.

WHEN OFFICERS ARRIVED ON SCENE, THEY HEARD DISTRESSING SOUNDS COMING FROM INSIDE THE RESIDENCE, GIVING THEM JUST CAUSE TO ENTER THE PREMISES. DURING THEIR SEARCH, THEY DISCOVERED TYLER (34) AND MAUREEN (31) HENDERSON IN THE LIVING ROOM UNDER THE INFLUENCE OF DRUGS, AND UPON CHECKING ONE OF THE BEDROOMS, DISCOVERED MICHAEL DUGGARD (26) AND SEAN BANCROFT (20) SODOMIZING AN INCAPACITATED DELILAH HENDERSON (9).

DUGGARD AND BANCROFT ALLEGED THAT THE ADULT HENDERSON'S KNEW WHAT WAS GOING ON IN THE ADJOINING ROOM AND THAT THEY PAID TYLE HENDERSON OVER $15,000 OVER THE COURSE OF THE LAST SIX MONTHS TO HAVE SEX WITH THEIR UNDERAGE DAUGHTER.

DELILAH HENDERSON PRESENTED TO RESPONDING OFFICERS WITH MULTIPLE BRUISES VISIBLE, GLASSY EYES, AND BLOOD ON HER BACKSIDE. LO MARKS AND JRO DUBRIS CALLED CHIEF JACKSON IMMEDIATELY AND REQUESTED AN IMMEDIATE TRANSPORT OF D.HENDERSON VIA AMBULANCE TO RADY CHILDREN'S HOSPITAL - SAN DIEGO.....

My body shakes and tears begin to well in my eyes as I continue to read through the report and discover that not only did my father *sell* my body to those disgusting men, but he sexually abused me right along with them. How could my biological mother have allowed this to happen to me, to her child, her little girl? How could my own father *do* those things to me?! And allow other men to do the same?! White hot rage courses through me as I continue to read all the horrific acts performed upon my young body. Even though I don't remember any of it—thank the Gods!—I can't seem to shake the connection to that version of me. Yes, she is me, but if I don't remember, do I have the right to be justifiably angry, especially at the humans whose faces I can't even conjure up an image of? With each turn of the report, the marks left on my body burn as I come to terms with how I acquired such scars.

I set the report aside with all the horrid details from the night my Dad—my REAL dad—took me to the hospital. The day that my life changed forever. I pick up the next file folder, this one with various sticky notes and flags sticking out from the sides. All the tiny paper flags have been smashed and bent into odd angles from being shoved into a tightly packed box. I take in a deep breath, fear racking my body at what information I might uncover as I continue to dig through this box. My hands tremble as I slip my fingers in between the folder cover and the first page. It feels like my entire life is resting on this moment. I have waited twenty-two years to learn about how I came into my parents' life, and this is it. This is the box of files that started it all.

I close my eyes and exhale, the deep breath sounding louder than it should with my entire apartment shrouded in anticipatory silence. The names *Henderson, Tyler* and *Henderson, Maureen* peek out from the next set of files. This is the file that holds the information on my biological parents. This will be the folder to answer who they were and why they would choose to do such atrocious things to me. It doesn't change a thing and I definitely wouldn't wish any different because I was granted the two most amazing parents any kid could have asked for. But to *finally* have all these missing pieces put together will be nice. I flip open the cover, open my eyes and look down at the twenty-six-year-old case file in front of me.

Staring up at me, with faces sunken in and skin dull and lifeless, are my biological parents. I cautiously run my fingers over their facial features. I share the same doe-shaped blue eyes as Maureen but my blond hair? That came from Tyler. The longer I stare at these photos, the more and more I can see myself in both of them. The high cheek bones from Maureen, the sharp jaw line from Tyler. I am the perfect amalgamation of my two parents. No. Not my parents. My two donors. They may have technically given me life and raised me—if you can even call it that—in my formative years, but my they were not my *parents*. I pull their paperclipped photos off the documents and start reading the case where this whole mess began.

CHAPTER TWENTY FIVE

I t doesn't take me long to read the entire folder on my birth parents and their heinous disregard for the life that they brought into this world. The drug trafficking Tyler was charged with pales in comparison to the shocking treatment I suffered at the hands of those that were supposed to protect and love me. My stomach churns at the thought of all the horrors this man inflicted upon me as a child. I'm not sure which is worse though: the fact that this man *sold me* and *used* me for his personal gain and sick satisfaction, or the fact that his *wife*—my so-called "mother"— sat there and was complicit in the whole thing. How can this human, this *woman*, who carried me in her womb have such a severe disregard of the life she nurtured for nine months?! And now I wonder if the abuse started as soon as I came home. The thought of an infant me being tortured makes my stomach churn. I toss the file unceremoniously onto the floor as unbridled fury and disgust fill my body anew. Could this case containing the dark secrets of a life I don't have any memories of get any worse?!

But alas, as I grumble and pull the next folder out of the cardboard box, I realize I really need to stop asking the Universe this question, because She seems to be having a blast showing me just how much worse things can get.

Chancler, Bradley.

I gasp in shock and horror when I see the name on the side. The folder drops from my hands with a *thud*. I feel ill.

After taking a moment to compose myself, I pick the file back up and find myself once again face-to-face with a grainy mugshot of Bradley Chancler, his deep-bronze tan and black hair unmarked by time. His chocolate-brown eyes hide dangerous secrets in the depths of them. My stomach lurches as I stare at this man, my mouth agape. I knew he was sent to prison for child sex trafficking when I looked him up in the system after his murder, but as I stare at his rap sheet it finally dawns on me that his file is in the same box as information on my apparent assault as a child. I pray to every God and Goddess that his dossier was placed here by accident but deep within my soul, I know that is just a pipe dream. Despite my better judgment, I continue to review his file.

As I read through the horrors of my life that have been shoved into boxes and simplified as notes, my stomach twists and turns into a thousand knots. The similarities between their deaths and how they tortured me as a child is uncanny. I finish off the last dossier on Mike and Sean—the latest murder victims and my neighbors!—and toss the file across the coffee table. It lands amongst the other thirty files that have been thrown around my tiny living room. I continue to stare at the jumble of files strewn across my floor, unable to comprehend what I have just read. I lean against my couch cushions, staring at the mess of papers, folders, and photos that litter my apartment. The overwhelming amount of information that I just consumed is starting to cause a massive migraine.

My phone dings as a news article flashes across my screen: *Two Hillcrest Men Found Dead in Gruesome Apartment Scene*

"That was quick to make headlines," I say out loud to no one. I trepidatiously click the notification, curious to see how much information could have possibly been put out in such a short amount of time. Seeing the deceased men's photos sends a horrific sensation through my spine, causing me to shudder and hold down a sick that threatens to overtake my entire body.

Union-Tribune

TWO HILLCREST MEN FOUND DEAD IN GRUESOME APARTMENT SCENE

SEAN BANCROFT, 46, AND MICHAEL "MIKE" DUGGARD, 52, FOUND DEAD BY LOCAL TEENAGER

SAN DIEGO - Late Monday night, two men were found brutally murdered in their apartment located at the 3900 block of 7th Avenue in Hillcrest.

At about 10 p.m., SDPD dispatch received a frantic call from Detective Delilah Jackson about a a gruesome scene in a tiny apartment in the Hillcrest Place Apartments. Police arrived on the scene just before 10:30 p.m. and refused to comment.

An informant let reporters for the San Diego Tribune know that the victims were Michael "Mike" Duggard, 52, and Sean Bancroft, 46. Both victims were stabbed repeatedly, *Dead Men Don't Rape* painted on their wall with their own blood.....

itness testimonies and police statements adorn the narrative, each piece of information a puzzle waiting to be solved. The authorities are searching for leads, and the city is holding its breath, gripped by the unsettling realization that danger can lurk around any corner.

Who the fuck released that information on their murders?! It hasn't even been twenty-four hours and they are already releasing very pertinent information on their demise. Who is the whistleblower, and how long until Captain Dubris loses his shit on said person?

Standing outside the light-yellow stucco house, I am hit with a sense of déjà vu. Something deep within the pit of my soul tells me I have been here before, but when, I can't be sure. This doesn't quite look like one of the houses I have been to before when called upon for a homicide. Despite the bright sun ahead, I feel no heat seeping into my bones. In fact, I can't even feel the grass beneath my bare feet. I am but a specter wherever my subconscious has landed me. My incorporeal form is weightless and unnoticed by the faceless figures walking around the street. A loud shrill breaks my thought process as I peer at my surroundings. My head snaps in the direction of the abode to my left where screams are emanating from behind the solid oak door, and I am suddenly transported into a tiny, filthy bedroom.

The stench of the room creeps up into my nostrils and I swallow down the burning bile threatening to upheave from my stomach. Fist-sized holes mar the dingy white walls, cigarette tar stains the ceiling which is covered in cobwebs. As I take in more of the squalid room, the feeling of being trapped and haunted settles into the recesses of my mind. Wherever this dream-state has transported me to, I cannot escape the heaviness that falls at my feet, planting me here.

"Momma, help me! Pleeeeeease!"

The familiar shriek lurches me out of my unease and my eyes finally fixate on the scene in front of me. On one end of the stained mattress kneels an emaciated woman, her hair in a tangled top knot upon her head, and at the other, a slender man with gaunt cheeks and a mess of blond hair. Between them, thrashing and wailing for help is a small child. My eyes bulge at the sight playing out before me, tears filling them to the brim with the realization.

"Hold the fuck still, you useless brat!" the man hollers, digging his knees deeper into the young girl's bare thighs. "I've warned you! Stop. Costing. Me. MONEY!"

As my own wails for him to stop pierce the air, they are drowned out by the little girl's shrieks of horror as a hot curling iron lashes away at her exposed body. My insides and thighs begin to burn as I sob and scream alongside the frail child in front of me, still unable to move. The longer I stare, the more realization sets in to what I am witnessing—again. This isn't just a horrible lucid dream that has been plaguing me for weeks on end.

I have been reliving all the horrible moments I went through as a child.

"Tyler, stop it!" I scream, finally unfrozen, and leap toward the abusive man as the world swirls around me, dropping me into the back of a sedan.

It's dark now and I'm greeted with a familiar yet fear-inducing smell. The overpowering scent of an exorbitant amount of overpriced cologne lingers in the air and assaults my nostrils as I see a large, dark figure in the front seat struggling with a smaller shadowed figure.

"You rotten bitch! I paid good money for you!"

Light suddenly illuminates the car with a quick flash from a lighter and the car is engulfed in the putrid smell of cigarettes. The red-hot cherry of a freshly lit cigarette seems to move of its own volition through the darkness above the front seats of the car. My eyes follow the flaming ember as it lowers toward the smaller of the two figures and quickly extinguishes, followed by a scream of pain. I grip at my stomach as the little girl's cries—my cries—fill the car, clenching my eyes shut to block out the pain burning at my flesh.

When I open my eyes, I have been transported once again, this time to a very expensive hotel room. Rich dark woods and deep-red sheets give the room a sense of opulence. A tall, fit, naked man has his back facing my spectral form. I am rooted in place again as I watch him take a fistful of the young girl's blond hair—no, my blond hair—and yank her head backward, spitting in her face. A slew of curses leave his lips as he throws the younger version of me across the floor.

Gods, why can't I just wake up?! Hot tears flow freely from my eyes as I watch the onslaught of violence against my younger self play out over and over again. Each scenario is a different horror I do not recall, and yet I feel so lucid in this moment. My younger self isn't even fighting back or crying anymore. My Gods, I can't be any more than seven or eight in these...memories? Flashbacks? What would I even consider these when I have had zero recollection of this happening to me until now? At least, not until I read that case file. I press my hands to my eyes hard enough to flash white. I'm screaming and crying for someone to help save the younger me even though I know help does eventually come, just way too late.

When I pull my palms from my eyes, I am in an entirely different area. The air around me reeks of Axe-body spray and suntan oil. I know this smell. This is the smell that has been haunting the hallways of my apartment building. The smell that crept over my skin and latched on at the non-consensual barrage of hands and mouths multiple times within the past month. And immediately I know that I am about to relive whatever nightmare Mike and Sean put me through as a small child. My body involuntarily begins to tremble and my stomach twists into a series of tightly woven knots. There I am, laying on the bed, my tiny, nine-year-old body naked and bloody with two grown men leering over me. Nine-year-old me has a face of stone, a thin line of drool pooling at the corner of my mouth from the drugs forced down my throat, a detail the toxicology report confirmed. My mind flashes back to the dossier on these two despicable humans and this is the day that I finally get the help I must have prayed for. I weep alongside the smaller version of myself as a single solitary tear falls *from the corner of her eye, across the bridge of her nose and onto the bed. Sean grabs the younger me by the ankles and yanks my limp body toward him, positioning me in a way that suits him.*

"No! No! STOP IT!" I manage to scream into the void just as he closes the gap between my naked body and his own. I lunge toward the duo, ready to strike and kick Sean away from the lifeless, adolescent me just as the room around me spins and flashes into bright white.

It takes a minute for my eyes to adjust to the blinding sunlight of this new scene where I see Jimmy yelling into his phone outside the precinct. I don't remember this. When did this happen?

"Hey Jimmy! Why don't you leave him alone? That man has bled for your right to be a douchebag. The least you could do is show him some respect," a familiar voice, my voice, echoes in this dream-like state.

Wait, I do remember this, but what in the world? Jimmy wasn't on his phone!

"Shut the fuck up, Jackson. Go do your weird locking fetish bullshit and mind your own business." He shoves his phone into his pocket, spinning on his heel and muttering words I didn't hear a few days ago, "Fucking bitch is off her goddamn rocker. I can't wait for her to slip up."

I clench my fists and grit my teeth, ready to swing at this specter form of my co-worker for his crude statements before the world dissolves around me and drops me into the back seat of a car.

I frantically look around as I hear a grown man's voice spewing curses at their black-clad passenger. I study the face of the shadowy figure next to me when I hear the driver speak again, his voice striking a familiar chord. It's Bradley!

"You sick fucking bastard!" he spits at his passenger. "You'll pay for that!"

The deafening crack of a bone breaking echoes through the car as the driver is hit with a handgun again. I blink and I am suddenly outside of the car, Bradley is now tied to his seat, and the shadowy figure is pouring gasoline all over his body. The sulfur strike of a match fills the air as the blackened figure drops it onto Bradley, his screams reverberating throughout the empty alleyway. I try to get a good look at the murderer as they turn in my direction. Before I can get a solid look at their face in the flickering back-alley light, the floor gives out from beneath me and I am dropped into the entrance of a different dark alleyway.

I give myself a moment to take in my surroundings. This is…This is the alley where Davit was murdered! I will my feet to rush to the area where Davit was found a few weeks ago. I'm not sure what I am hoping to accomplish by racing toward something that has already happened. Either way, I reach his final resting place just as the shadowy figure stomps on the back of his head repeatedly.

"Hey! Stop!" I scream, my voice sounding like it's underwater and garbled.

The dark figure turns to look in my direction as if they hear me and just before I can get a glimpse of their face, everything fades to black and the quiet of the alley is replaced with the maniacal, soft laughter of men and the familiar sound of an outdated dryer. Once again, I take a moment to observe the space around me and see everything where it should be in my apartment complex laundry room—and the unforgettable smell of cheap, spray-on deodorant and suntan oil.

Oh Gods.

Am I about to watch Sean and Mike start the assault that I'm fairly certain they finished on the steps of my dads' house?

It's okay. It's okay. I tell myself repeatedly. Jericho will come. Jericho will save me in this dream-state just like he did when I was pinned against those dryers not that long ago. But as their hands continue roaming my body, there is no Jericho. No savior to stop this.

Out of the corner of my eye, I notice the other me reach up and grab Mike's hand, savagely twisting it away from my small frame. My doppelgänger's face is hard as stone, her nails digging into the man's exposed flesh.

"I said don't. Touch. Me," she growls.

Mike yanks his hand out of her grasp, clutching at his wrist. "Still just as ornery, I see. We were just leaving anyway," he says in a gruff voice. "Come see us if you ever want to try again," Mike calls out before he disappears around the corner.

I stare in abject horror. Where's Jericho?! This isn't how I remember this happening!

A quick spin of the room and the scenery violently shifts to Dads' house. I'm staring down the old wooden stairs watching as Mike and Sean grope me all over. Their fingers and mouths roaming where they shouldn't. But my doppelgänger isn't moving. She's not making a sound. I am, however. The real me. This me. I am shaking as tears pour down my face, my incorporeal form frozen in terror and unheard screams of pain escaping my lips. I think I'm going to be sick. This fucked up journey through my past traumas that my consciousness is taking me on is gut-wrenching and nauseating.

I don't think I can do this.

I don't think I can take this.

I clench my eyes closed as sirens sound softly in the distance. Help is arriving for that version of me at least. I know what happens next. Rita will come storming through the door and start yelling at the junior officer questioning me the way he is. The amount of police that invaded my father's home that day because of me both sickens and saddens me. Officers traipse up and down the stairs, walking right through me. A reminder that I am but a ghost floating through fleeting memories. I watch as the officers search every area of my father's house, and out of the corner of my eye I catch a glimpse of where I last saw the boxes that are now littering my apartment floor.

There was no bloody hand print on it! What the hell?!

The entire world lurches around me again with a pull from my belly button before I can get a better look at the box left at the top of the stairs. Vomit threatens to escape my body as I'm dropped into an area filled with loud, ear-piercing music. The room around me is cloaked in darkness that seems to suffocate every ray of light. The air is thick with a putrid stench, metal, booze, and body odor assaulting my senses and making it difficult to breathe. Each breath I take is a struggle, the foul odor clawing its way into my lungs like tendrils of death. I can feel my skin crawl with revulsion as the smell seeps into every pore, filling me with a sense of dread and despair.

In this blackened chamber of horrors, I am consumed by a primal fear, unable to see what lurks in the shadows but acutely aware of its malevolent *presence. The darkness seems to pulsate with a life of its own, whispering twisted secrets and haunting me with nightmarish visions. My heart pounds in my chest like a drumbeat of terror, each thud beating in time with the heavy music assaulting my ears. My senses heighten as I strain to make sense of the chaos around me. Voices rise in anger, sharp and cutting.*

The sounds of a struggle ring out through the darkness, the harsh impact of flesh against flesh reverberating through the empty space. Guttural grunts and desperate pleas form a cacophony of conflict that wraps me in its suffocating embrace. I can't see the faces of those who are fighting, but their voices paint a vivid picture of pain and desperation. Anger mingles with fear, the emotions raw and unfiltered in the darkness. My heart races with unease as I listen to the violent symphony unfolding before me, the primal instinct to flee warring with the morbid curiosity that binds me to this nightmarish scene.

Just as my eyes begin to adjust to the darkness, a door to another room opens and light pours in, nearly blinding me. In that split second of illumination, I see Mike, now a eunuch and lying in a pool of his own blood. Sean screams into the pitch blackness of the room that is consuming both of us, threatening to fight whomever is hiding in the shadows. A thud signals that Sean has collapsed to the floor and as my eyes adjust to the darkness once more, I squint to make out the figure moving about the room. Finally, I catch a glimpse of the mysterious figure who is responsible for the onslaught of murders that have terrorized my city.

My eyes fly open with a start and I'm left disoriented and gasping for breath. A glance out my window reveals the hazy glow of the setting sun only slightly muted by my curtains. As I struggle to shake off the remnants of the nightmare, the details begin to blur, but the lingering unease clings to my consciousness. I look around, seeking solace in the familiar objects that adorn the room—a worn-out blanket draped over the back of the couch, a forgotten cup of water on the coffee table. Even the blood-stained boxes and file folders tossed unceremoniously around my tiny apartment.

The blood-stained boxes that weren't blood-stained in whatever night-marish memory recall I just went through.

The soft gleam of light from the microwave numbers creates shape-shifting shadows in the corner of my eye. I pour a glass of water, the cool liquid soothing the hoarseness of my aching throat. Leaning against the kitchen counter, I stare into the fading light of dusk as it falls just beyond the window, trying to calm my breathing that quickens with every passing second. As I gaze into the living room from my spot in the kitchen, a sickening sensation creeps up from the depths of my gut. It feels like a storm raging within me, threatening to spill its contents at any moment. The taste of bile rises in the back of my throat, bitter and overwhelming. My head swims with dizziness, the world tilting and spinning around me in a nauseating whirl. Each breath is a struggle, as if the air itself has turned thick and heavy with the promise of impending sickness.

I clutch my abdomen, trying in vain to quell the rising tide of nausea that threatens to overwhelm me. But the queasiness only intensifies, a relentless onslaught that leaves me feeling weak and helpless. I close my eyes, willing the sensation to pass to no avail.

I race to the bathroom, emptying the contents of my stomach into the toilet. My whole world begins to crash around me. The flashbacks and screaming little girl I have been hearing for these last few weeks was *me*. My brain has been trying to help me remember and it wasn't until Bradley, Davit, Mike, and Sean were murdered that my body finally relaxed. It wasn't until this nightmare seeped out of the deepest recesses of my brain that I knew the truth, that I knew who murdered the four men. The monster that committed such heinous acts, throwing San Diego into panic as the murders got worse and worse.

That the monster is me.

CHAPTER TWENTY SIX

I don't understand how I could not remember committing any of those horrific crimes, or how I was hiding all the evidence. How was I never caught on any CCTV footage or seen by witnesses? And if I saw Jericho at every crime scene and even remember him saving me in the laundry room...where was he in the flashback to that memory? Why would my brain conjure up Jericho as my savior in that moment when it was really me?

My body convulses uncontrollably as my stomach rebels, forcing its contents upward with a violent surge. The taste of bile fills my mouth as wave after wave of nausea wracks my shuddering form and I retch into the toilet again. The bile is hot and burning and produces a feeling different from all the times I threw up my food in the prior days. There's no stopping it now. My throat burns with each heave, the muscles contracting in a painful rhythm as my body tries to purge itself of the realization that has been thrust upon me. I continue to gag, feeling every muscle in my body strain with the effort. The sound is primal and raw, echoing off the walls around me in a sickening serenade of shame. Tears stream down my cheeks as I gasp for breath between spasms, my entire being consumed by the overwhelming urge to expel everything my body contains. Finally, it subsides, leaving me trembling and exhausted. The worst is over, at least for now. I slump against the cold floor, completely spent, dried streaks of tears staining my cheeks. I snag some toilet paper, wiping the sick from underneath my nose as I stare out of the bathroom door, trying to focus on the scene in the distance.

I stumble out of the bathroom and back to my living room, plopping onto the edge of my couch. Tears continue to stream down my face as I sit among the sea of case files that document how horribly I was mistreated as a small child. My entire body shakes at the realization of what I have done. How do I come back from this? I can't just sweep it under the rug. I refuse to become another statistic where cops get away with shit with only a slap on the wrist.

No.

I have to tell someone.

My train of thought is interrupted by a knock at the door and my head instantly snaps up toward the noise. My heart leaps into my throat as the unexpected sound of visitors permeates the silence of my home. Panic floods my senses, my mind racing to comprehend the intrusion. Who could it be at this hour, and why? Every nerve in my body tingles with apprehension as I approach the door, my footsteps hesitant and slow. I carefully tiptoe around all the papers strewn across my floor and press my face to the peephole. I see Captain Dubris and Rita standing outside my apartment. A torrent of emotions courses through me. I haven't seen the captain since he came to console me after the funeral and the last time I saw Rita was outside the crime scene at my apartment complex the other night.

I take a deep breath, holding it in to make a feeble attempt at calming the anxiety attack building within me. With trembling hands, I reach out to grasp the handle, the metallic coldness sending a shiver down my spine. I swallow hard as I open the door.

"Good evening, Delilah," Captain Dubris offers the first greeting as soon as my face appears through the crack in the door. "I hope we're not disturbing you at this late hour. May we come in?"

I nervously glance behind me at all the old case files—*my* case files—scattered across the floor. I sigh and hang my head as I usher them inside. A quick look at their faces tells me their visit isn't going to bring good news and with the way they're eyeing all the files, I feel this is my end. Did they already know what I only just discovered about myself? The sound from closing my apartment door seems to reverberate off of my walls.

"Can I offer y'all anything to drink?" I anxiously stride over to my small kitchen, pulling out cups before they can answer. My heart starts to thump loudly and I wonder if the captain and Rita can hear it.

"That-that won't be necessary," Captain Dubris's words are soft and uncertain. Rita hasn't said a word and will not look at me. She's always been a hard one to read.

"Oh. What did y'all need?" I place the cups on the counter, not meeting their eyes. I can feel them boring into me and my stomach drops. I steal a glance in their direction and I see Rita scanning the files that litter my living room.

"I found those in my Dad's attic and then with the assault I just forgot! Then I found them outside my apartment today and curiosity got the best of me! I meant to return them but—"

Captain holds his hand up to silence me and I shrink into myself. My cheeks flush at the feeling of being scolded by the last father figure I have on this planet. The disappointment in his eyes eats away at what little self-esteem I have left. Without saying a word, Captain Dubris motions for us to take a seat in my messy living room where I have spent the last few hours reliving my worst nightmares.

"All right, listen up," he says, his voice low but commanding. "I've been through every detail, every scrap of evidence we've got. You're not going to like it, but you need to hear it. So pay attention."

I nod, trying to steady my breathing. I have to keep it together. Maybe they don't actually know what I now know. Maybe they will verify that Jericho is a real person and he's the one who's done all of these gruesome things. Maybe my brain is catastrophizing from everything that has happened and I'm now in some weird fever dream, still lying in that hospital bed.

"First thing—" He pulls a file from under his arm that I didn't notice when he first arrived and drops it on top of the files that are still on the table. The folder lands with a deafening thud. "—we've finally got the security footage from outside the bar where Bradley was burned alive. It's clear. You can see a glimpse of the assailant leaning against the corner of the building around one fifty-five a.m., right before the incident. And I'm talking right before. They look over their shoulder, wait a few seconds, and then can be seen pulling their jacket tighter against their body before following behind Chancler as he leaves the bar."

I feel the hairs on the back of my neck prickle. I have always been told to trust my instincts, but this...this isn't sitting right. I distinctly remember seeing Jericho running by the alleyway when we were called out to investigate.

"Now," Captain Dubris continues, flipping open the file, "we ran the prints from Chancler's door. His prints—clear as day. But here's the kicker: those weren't the only prints on the handle. You see this?" He flips to a photograph of a handprint, smeared but unmistakable. "We also found prints from someone else. Someone who shouldn't have been there."

I swallow hard, trying to push back the cold creeping up my spine. "Who was it?"

He doesn't answer. Instead, he flips through the file and starts another long-winded explanation. "The next murder, Davit Petrosyan. Murdered behind his restaurant. Same words written near the crime scene that were at Bradley's: *Dead Men Don't Rape*. Oddly enough, there weren't any cameras pointing in this alleyway, but the writing at both murder scenes was identical."

He takes a breath before he adds, "The next part of this gets uglier. The murders have now been brought to your doorstep."

I try to swallow the lump in my throat, but it's stuck there. "The murder I stumbled upon and called in," I mutter, barely recognizing my own voice.

Captain Dubris nods slowly. "That's right. And you gave the dispatcher the same words that were at the other crime scenes: *Dead Men Don't Rape*. Except, you can't see those words from the open door. Which makes all this even more complicated."

I blink rapidly, fighting the rush of panic threatening to break through. I don't know what to say. The walls feel like they are closing in, and the silence between us is suffocating. I very distinctly remember seeing the words on the wall from the doorway. There is no way I just dreamt that up, did I?

"So, now," Captain Dubris says, pushing the file toward me, "you've got a decision to make. Either you help me connect the rest of these dots, or you're gonna get swept up in the tide. Either way, we're not done."

I stare down at the file. My heart races. This isn't just an investigation anymore—it is my life on the line. And somewhere, in the back of my mind, I know the captain isn't just talking about the case. I stare blankly at my mentor, a man I have come to admire greatly, and then at my partner for over a decade. I am completely dumbfounded and have no idea how to respond to either of them. I close my eyes, silent tears making their way down my cheeks.

He is talking about me.

He knows.

"Delilah, there's no easy way to say this," Captain straightens up, his authority radiating off of him. "You are under arrest for the murders of Bradley Chancler, Davit Petrosyan, Michael Duggard, and Sean Bancroft."

DEAR READER,

Thank you so much for traveling through the breaking psyche of Delilah Jackson. While I know this book involves a lot of dark themes, it has been quite cathartic to write and help with my own PTSD. The experiences of depersonalization, OCD, and the disordered eating are written based off of my own experiences with these mental health disorders. Please know and understand that people with the same diagnoses all present differently and handle their trauma differently. For me, I wrote to seek a justice I have never received and will never receive.

I want to send a never ending *thank you* to my amazing friends and family for sticking by me through all the ups and downs of writing my first full length novel as well as helping me through my healing journey decades in the making. To my partners: thank you for the late night, incoherent talks and picking me up when I laid in the bed crying over my writing when the pain of reliving my most traumatic moments became too much. I love you both to the moon and back and twice around the sun.

To my wonderful editor, Haleigh of Page Perfectors. Without whom this manuscript would not be as polished and coherent as it is today.

If you enjoyed Delilah's story, please feel free to leave a review on Amazon, GoodReads, or wherever you digitally log your book progress.

Remember: you are important. I see you, and I hear you.

Your Partner in Crime,

ABOUT THE AUTHOR

30something year old, neurospicy, chronically ill, queer, mother of 4 living her best life in rural Southern California. By day she is a virtual English tutor and by night she is mother, author, and cozy game streamer and content creator. Along side her sister, Becca Lynne also owns a homemade witchy and mythological candle shop called Lore of the Pomegranate.

Check out Becca Lynne's other works on her website or wherever books are sold.